A Memory of Flowers and Coconut

Short Stories

Raywat Deonandan

IntanjiblePublishing

Intanjible Publishing

Reviews of Raywat Deonandan's Fiction

- "The imagery is often quite wonderful, capturing sights, sounds, smell, touch, very well. The cultural nuances, especially the difficulty of 'bridging' two or more societies, are subtle yet sensitive." -Linda Field, *Arsenal Pulp Press* (Victoria, B.C.)

- "[Deonandan] has a gift for strong characterization and sardonic humour, two elements I find important for good fiction." -Kim McDougall, *Morgan House Publishing* (Valleyfield, Quebec)

- "Through [Deonandan's] brilliant characterization and dialogue, the reader is engaged in continuous storying... Auxiliary characters become a vital part of the story as well." -Anne Forsythe-Moore, *Canadian Author Magazine* (London, Ontario)

- "Although [Deonandan's] language is heavy handed compared to the now ubiquitous minimalist jargon, it works quite well." -C. Baba, *Printed Matter* (Tokyo, Japan)

- "Quirky and engaging." -Jim Bartley, *The Globe and Mail* (Toronto, Ontario)

- "Here comes a young writer, crossing your path almost noiselessly, who tells stories in such an unpretentious fashion that one is left wondering about the unbearable lightness of his craftsmanship." -Harald Leusmann, *The Caribbean Writer* (Muncie, Indiana)

- "Deonandan celebrates the dignity of the common people." -Barbara Mujica, *Americas Magazine* (Washington, DC)

- "[Deonandan] makes a clarion call for a return to

origins, to the times of the beginnings, which will restore the possibility of permanent happiness and freedom." -Indira Rampersad, *University of the West Indies*

This Volume's Publication History

1. **Midnight Shift**

Originally published in *Toronto Noir* (New York: Akashic Books, © 2008)

2. **A Memory of Flowers and Coconut**

Originally published in *Pagitica Magazine* (Toronto, © 2002)

3. **Destroyer of Worlds**

Originally published in *Desilicious* (Toronto: Arsenal Pulp Press, © 2003)

4. My Girlfriend's Tattoo
Originally published in *Tatmag* (Toronto, ©1993)

5. New
Previously unpublished © 2009

6. Besting Death
Previously unpublished © 2008

7. Lords of Izzat
Previously unpublished © 2006

8. Rupinder
Previously unpublished © 2009

9. The Nadan's New Clothes
Previously unpublished © 2009

10. Drawing Dead People
Previously unpublished © 2000

11. The Inviolate Rectitude of Human Life
Previously unpublished © 1994

12. **The Emerald in The Diamond**

Originally published in *Green's Magazine* (Saskatoon, © 1994)

In the past, I've dedicated my books to my parents, my siblings, and even my students. I'm rather giddy that this is my first opportunity to dedicate a personal work to my son, who will turn five this year. While these stories represent, in large part, memories of the distant past, perhaps he will one day take an interest in my memories and therefore in his own heritage.

Contents

Chapter One

Midnight Shift

"Over here," Meera said, taking Yanni by the hand and dragging him down a freshly mopped corridor. It stank of ammonia, an antiseptic nasal assault that held a warped erotic appeal for some among the stethoscope and lab coat set. Meera drew Yanni's mouth to hers and tasted of his youth, inhaling his masculine scents and flavours.

"Slow down," Yanni whispered. "And be quiet. Someone will hear!"

"Wimp," Meera chastised, running her dark hands under Yanni's loosened shirt. "There are only two nurses on this floor, and they're both at the station." Yanni still hesitated. "Besides," Meera continued, "Maybe you want to get caught?" She grinned in her devilish way and pinched his nipple, pushing Yanni against the sterile white wall.

He was yielding to her touch, soft clay beneath her will-ful hands. Meera pressed him against the sign that read, "2nd Floor, Rheumatology". The irony was not lost on her, as they strived to express an act of guileless youth in a place of broken agedness. The odours of imposed steril-ity, the colours of bureaucratic lifelessness and joyless dull lights --these were tokens of a philosophy that pushed aside the ardour of youth, the mystic charms of sex and dirty, musical physicality. It was as if she and Yanni were conse-crating lifeless dry-wall with their hot, staccato breaths, all the time mildly aware of the clicking heels of the midnight nursing shift a hallway away, and of the almost impercep-tible groans of the elderly patients swimming in their beds, wracked by dreams impossible for naive, young medical residents to comprehend.

They clutched each other in that particular desperate way, with each muscle seemingly simultaneously shocked and delighted that it had been recruited to such a pleasant purpose, and melted into the slow rhythm of human inti-macy. The barren hospital corridor seemed less foreboding now that their eyes became accustomed to the darkness. At the end of the hall, a small window was open, letting in dull sounds from University Avenue below: a rushing stream of honking taxis, whooshing motorcycles, traffic lights hooting and chirping for the blind, and the chatter of the occasional passersby.

"Come on," Yanni said, spinning from the wall and dragging Meera by her stethoscope. He pulled her into one of the empty patient rooms and onto a bed. The tightly tucked hospital sheets were a cliche, one that made them both chuckle as they gave up trying to get under them. Then they heard a noise.

"Who is there?" It was a man's voice, weak and desperate.

Yanni sprung to his feet, letting his open shirt fall back into place. "I'm Dr. Rostoff. This is Dr. Rai. Who are you?" Meera clicked on the room light, revealing an elderly man in the room's secondary bed. "This room is supposed to be empty."

"Manoj Persaud," the man said, looking pleadingly at Meera, perhaps finding solace in a face as brown as his own. Yanni snatched the man's chart, flipping through the long paper sheets with the guilty anger of one interrupted in a moment of intimacy.

Yanni frowned. "Meera, he's supposed to be in the Latner Centre." He whispered: "Palliative care."

"I know I dyin'," Manoj Persaud said weakly in a slight Caribbean accent. "Na need fo' whisper." He pulled himself to a sitting position on the bed, revealing striped pyjamas and furry pink slippers with bunny ears. Meera smiled at the sight. "One dem volunteer been give me," Persaud said, gesturing to the slippers. "When I dead, you can tek 'em."

Meera sat next to the strange man and started with the usual doctor routine: the pulse check, the pen light in the pupils, the incomprehensible examination of the mouth and tongue. Persaud pushed her away. "What you doin', child?" He demanded, then coughed brackishly. "I said I dyin'. You go find somethin' new fo' kill me faster?"

Yanni dropped the file onto the bed and sighed. "Mr. Persaud, you are 88 years old and suffering from several very serious medical conditions. I don't know how you got to this floor or this room, but we have to get you back to the Latner Centre right away. They can take care of you better. We just don't have the facilities..."

"Boy," Persaud coughed. "I come down here because he comin' for me. He go get me sometime soon, but he kyaan do it now. Na now. He got fo' wait till me ready. I got fo' hide, just fo' tonight. Just until m' can tell somebody m' story."

"Who?" Meera implored, stroking the old man's face and feeling cold, wet fatigue. "Who's coming for you?"

Persaud's eyes widened and his jaw dropped. He leaned forward and beckoned her closer. The room seemed to darken then, with the hum of the old ceiling fan fading into the ether, and a taste of slightly stale honey upon the air. "Yahhhm," Persaud said, in all solemnity. "Yahhhm come fo' me."

Yanni frowned, but Meera motioned him back. "Yama," she explained. "The Hindu god of death."

"Yes, Mr. Persaud," Yanni said. "I'm sorry, but death is coming. For all of us. For you sooner, though. I'm sorry. Which is why it's important...."

"Shut up, boy," Persaud said sharply to Yanni, then turned to Meera, cupping her heart-shaped face in his spotted hands. "You undahstand, right? Yahhhm come fo' me, fo' tek m' soul. And da all right, child. Da all right. Is okay. But na now! Na right now! Not before m' can tell you why Yahhhm come fo' me personally."

Yanni pushed his hand through his thick blonde hair and sighed again. Typically, rheumatology rotation didn't involve psychiatric consults, but the midnight shift was famous for its many exceptions. And psychiatric issues were certainly not unknown to downtown Toronto hospitals. He reached for the phone by the bed, but Persaud intercepted with his skeletal hand.

"Boy. Please listen." Persaud's eyes were those of a doomed beast, pleading upward from the abatoir floor. "Yahhhm is comin' here. Tonight. Right now." His eyes slowly drifted to the hallway, to the open window at the end. Instantly, from the street below, there was a loud smashing noise, followed immediately by the sickly sound of bending metal and the unmistakable screams of humans in distress.

Yanni and Meera raced to the window. From the other end of the hallway, the shift nurses were also running to windows, so loud was the noise. Down below, like a report from the evening news of any unnamed metropolitan centre, a scene of traffic horror unfolded. Two delivery trucks had collided and were blocking traffic on all six lanes of University Avenue, sprawling across the pedestrian median and even knocking down one of the ghastly statues that usually stood watch. One truck was on fire, and police and fire engines were miraculously already on the scene. No casualties could be seen through the press of onlookers, who continued to stream in from the throngs occupying nearby Queen Street, likely drawn by sounds of disaster; but no doubt the Emergency Room below would soon be pressed into duty. It was an excellent ER, Meera knew; one of the best in the country. Still, a part of her wondered if she should rush down to help.

Persaud coughed loudly and beckoned them to the bed. Meera came back to his side. "Yahhhm," he said, as if in explanation. "Death comin'. Na got too much time. Got fo' tell you m' story first!"

"Look at all the people down there!" Yanni called from the window, amazed by the streams of late-night disaster voyeurs descending on this otherwise unpopular street. I know it's a horrible thing, and I hope everyone's all right. But what a show it must be on the ground!"

Persaud stroked Meera's face then fondled her stethoscope. "You so young to be among we so old," he said. "And dis," he showed her the end of the stethoscope. "Dis does give you comfort? You med'cine kyaan stop Yahhhm when Yahhhm want fo' come." He grinned an awful toothless grin that slitted his yellowing eyes and widened his gaping nostrils. But there was nonetheless something attractive and familiar about him. "How old you be, child?"

Meera said nothing.

"Is okay," Persaud said. "No need fo' answer. You daddy dead, right?" She nodded, almost zombie-like in her silence. "Is okay," he soothed. "We all got fo' dead. Is okay." Meera's face hardened. Whatever slight spell the strange old man had cast on her was now fading, chased off by the invocation of her father's sacred memory.

"Dr. Rostoff is right," Meera said. "We have to get you back to your room. Then we'd better go to Emergency to see if we're needed."

Persaud's lips tightened and he studied her carefully. Then he turned to Yanni, who was still bewitched by the scene of carnage on the street. "You, boy! Tell me you see Yahhhm."

"What?" Yanni, annoyed, waved Persaud away. But, nevertheless, he looked through the throngs on the street. To a man, each was enthralled with the heroic acts of fire fighters hosing down flaming trucks and pulling bodies from crushed vehicles. But there was one...

Persaud called to Yanni. "You see him, na? Tell me!"

Yanni was silent. But he kept his eye on this one special man on the street, this one man who was not watching the carnage. Instead, he was looking up, directly at the window from which Yanni now peered.

"Describe he!" Persaud ordered. But Yanni remained silent. The watcher continued to stand apart from the crowd, his hands in his jacket pockets, locking eyes with Yanni. Yanni's fingers yellowed as they gripped the window sill a tad more tightly than was comfortable, but he snorted dismissively at the watcher.

Meera gazed back at her friend and colleague, and was at a loss. She was torn in many directions, ripped apart like one of the vehicles in the crash. Competing responsibilities and desires jockeyed for priority. Yet the balance of her focus remained on the strange old man in the bed next to her.

"You is Indian," Persaud said. "You go undahstand. Dat is why you been sent fo' hear m' story."

Meera shook her said slowly. "Mr. Persaud..." She paused, knowing that further appeals for him to return to palliative care would be met with stolid refusal. And with the emergency outside, it was unlikely she would find sufficient help to move him against his will; not without sedating him.

She fell into his gaze, so sad yet intense. His yellow fish-like eyes bent into that sad puppy-like configuration, and the spotted skin on the sides of his face drooped in its losing struggle against time and gravity. He looked so familiar, so sadly familiar. "I'm not Indian," she said. "Well, I'm of Indian descent; but I was born in Kenya and grew up here in Toronto..."

"Doesn't mattah," Persaud said, shaking his head forcefully. "You is Indian. Like I. Me been born in Guyana. Never been see India." His accent seemed to thicken as the evening progressed. But Meera had no trouble following. His gravitas commanded complete focus and understanding. "Never been see India," he said again. "Don't know m' caste or m' daddy's caste. But I is a pandit just the same. One priest of God!"

Meera reflected, was tempted to smile. Her own father, whom this man so wished to resemble, had hated religion.

He had refused to raise his children with religion, had thrown his wife's idols from the home, and had famously quipped, "When things go well, we thank the gods. But when things go to hell, we blame everybody but the gods! What bullshit is this?" But in the end, even he had asked for a priest.

"You were a pandit in Guyana?" She asked him.

"Yes," Persaud said. His face darkened and his eyes deepened. The sounds of the street seemed to retreat then, isolating Meera alone with the old man, cushioned from Yanni, the window and the rest of the world. "I is a pandit now, and I was a pandit then." He paused and stared at her meaningfully. "I was a pandit of Kali." He spat the last word.

Again, Meera smiled. "I didn't know Kali was so popular outside India."

"Kali be another face of the same God," Persaud said, screwing up his own wizened face in mock dismissal of her seeming ignorance. "Goddess of blood, she. Goddess of glorious bittah red wine that pump in we veins. She scare the white people, na. But we know: she be a mama just like any lady. We respect mama. We respect daddy. And when you is a slave or servant in the cane fields of Guyana --back when the white man tek all you history, all you possessions, all you beliefs and give you Jesus Christ instead-- when you is a slave or a servant you need cling to you mama and you daddy with greater force!" His gaze intensified, as did his hold on Meera's hand. "Because dat is all you got, in the end. Dat is all you got."

It was then that Meera noticed Yanni was being uncharacteristically quiet. She looked to him and saw only his back, with his untucked plaid shirt whipping in the wind from the window. "Yanni," she asked, "Are you all right?"

"He's just staring up at me," Yanni said. He continued to look down into the melee below, red and yellow flashing sirens reflecting off his expressionless face.

"Yahhhm," Persaud intoned. "Tell dis old man, please, boy. How the god of death look? He tall? He old or he young? How black is he face? When he come, I go not see he. He go tek m' soul and I go not see he face."

Yanni replied without intonation, only fact. "He's about 21, five foot eight, but quite heavy-set, wearing a white-and-blue University of Toronto jacket. And he's b lond... and white." Persaud jerked at the last. "Maybe he's just catatonic. Or in shock. All he does is stare up at me; at this window. Maybe he needs a doctor."

Meera squeezed Persaud's hand, then stood up. "Yanni," she said. "It's time we went to work. Let's send for a wheel-chair to take Mr. Persaud back to palliative, then you and I had better report to Emergency. You think?"

Yanni detached himself from the window and scratched his head. "Sure, M. Let's go."

"Wait!" Persaud bellowed. "Listen! All me need is ten minute. Just listen a m' story fo' ten minute then you can do what the hell you want fo' do. Yahhhm go come before ten minute. Just listen a m' story, na. I got fo' tell somebody before me dead, or Kali go cuss m' soul." He stared at the two of them for a good long couple of heartbeats. "You want she fo' cuss m' soul? No? Good. Come listen, na."

Yanni made an odd dismissive noise and returned to his post by the window, voyeuristically surveying the crowd. Sheepishly, Meera returned to Persaud's side, an imploring look in her eyes. "Okay," she said. "Tell me. But then we have to take you back to your own room."

And Manoj Persaud launched into his tale...

It was years before Guyana had obtained its political independence from Britain. The decades that had passed of slavery for the Blacks, near genocide for the Natives and of indentured service for the Indians had bred a thirst for release from the chains of colonial rule. With each layer of Europeanness painted atop this weather-beaten Asian and African tapestry came a strengthening of its foreign matte, a calling for connections to lives and philosophies left centuries and fathoms away. African animism, sporadic puddles of voodoo, the naturalistic magics of the scattered Native tribes, and the myriad faiths smuggled from India all found fertile soil in this wet chasm of discontent. Amongst the Indian immigrants, the cult of Kali was revived and flourished.

In the telling of the tale, Persaud gurgled and his words took on a distant tenor. "Goddess Kali," he whispered. "Omnipotent power absolute. She be the origin of cosmos and spirit. Deity of time, eternity and source of all energies. Kali bless us and we triumph over evil, destroy rogues and knaves, expel inauspicious souls and repel demons." He focused on Meera again, slowly intoning, "She be knowledge. She be bliss."

Meera felt the dying man's pulse again, worried for his stress. She opened her mouth to speak, but Persaud covered it with his quivering hand. "Let me finish, na. You got fo' undahstand. The white man, he afeared o' Kali. He think she be demonic, wit' blood and scariness. But dat is fo' he. Kali is we mama. She be the female face of God, the angry mama who does protect she piknee, she children. We is she children. It is –what you say?––a metaphor. We weak before the white man, so we need one strong image of we mama for protection. You see?"

Meera nodded. And Persaud continued his narration...

Manoj Persaud had been a priest at the temple of Kali, where scores of devotees came weekly, sometimes daily, to offer obeisance to the mother goddess. In exchange, they received stable employment, healthy children, enough food to last the month, or whatever else it was they prayed for. It was Persaud who interpreted the omens and prodigies, who interceded between mortals and goddess. It was Persaud who interpreted the lost ways of obscure India to the subcontinent's forgotten and wretched Caribbean progeny.

But tensions were mounting as demands for political independence grew louder on the streets, in the newspapers, the rum shops and even within the temples. "And one day," Persaud said, "dem been come fo' talk wit' me." Six men they were, regular devotees of Kali, some even Persaud's relatives. They abased themselves before the priest and asked for a special puja, a special divine way or ceremony, for Kali to guarantee and accelerate Guyana's impending independence.

"I tell dem fo' pray and fo' make sacrifice to Kali, like dem always do, wit' coins, food and fasting," Persaud said, a sense of both sadness and horror growing behind his eyes. "But dem say dem want something extra. Something more. Fo' Kali. Fo' big big magic."

The younger Persaud had watched his devotees with growing unease, as the full extent of their petition came to be understood. For a boon of this magnitude, one affecting a whole nation of people, the old ways would have required a human sacrifice. But modern times employed modern methods, with pumpkins standing in for human heads; or the use of human effigies constructed of flour and mud, slashed with razor sharp machetes. Persaud presented these tamer options to his petitioners.

"But dem know the magic," he said with growing weariness. "Dem know the sacrifice, how the sacrifice must be aware. It must know it own fate and not be acting to stop the cutlass." Only then would the magic work, when the ultimate unseemly price had been paid. Only then would Kali grant them their wish.

Meera grew pale with the unfolding of the tale. Like a journey taken on a cloudy morning, its horrifying destination was rapidly becoming clearer as more steps were taken. Persaud's face was pleading, almost desperate with apology. "No," he said. "I not want fo' do dat! I tell dem. Dis pandit does not hold wit' dem old ways!"

But he had to tell them something. If he just sent them away, who knew what atrocity they would enact? Perhaps they would kidnap some poor fool and murder him sloppily in their own faulty, homemade Kali puja, accomplishing nothing except creating misery for all involved-- and offending God in every way possible.

"So I tell dem," Persaud said. "I tell dem: it must be a white child. Dem must kill one white child." He sat back against the wall, grinding his gums, waiting for Meera to react. But there was only silence. Meera regarded him with a strange detachment, struggling to balance horror with pity and disgust. She felt herself slide backwards, her hands near her face.

Persaud leaned forward again. "Undahstand! You got fo' undahstand! Where dem stupid boys go find one white child? We never see no white piknee. Only white man wit' he gun, he whip and he stick. Where dem skinny brown village boys go get one white child? I been tryin' fo' save dem, see? I been tryin' fo' prevent dem doin' some damn stupidness!"

Persaud's eyes exploded into tears. They rushed like torrents down his cheeks and into the sides of his huffing mouth. His breathing was shallow and forced, wheezing at times between bouts of fitful, pathetic wailing. "I been tryin' fo' mek dem task impossible," he whispered into the tissues Meera was using to wipe his face.

"But it wasn't impossible," Meera asked cautiously. "Was it?"

At that, Persaud reached into the front pocket of his pyjama pants and pulled out a crumpled, yellowed piece of newsprint. Meera took it and unfolded it. On the top it read, "Stabroek News, Georgetown, Guyana". The date was 1961. It was a news story about the disappearance of the baby daughter of the overseer of a sugar cane plantation in rural Guyana. Her name was Helen and her surname was seemingly Dutch. There was no photo, but Meera could assume the girl was white.

"My God," she said aloud. "They found one." Persaud nodded and sobbed. "But how can you be sure they killed her? Or that they were the ones who killed her?"

Persaud lay back against the headboard of the bed, spent. His face glistened with tears and sweat and his head now resembled a desiccated brown skull. He seemed to be ageing before Meera's very eyes. Unexpectedly, he smiled in that sad, dejected but resigned way that the elderly sometimes do. "I know," he said, "because dem been bring me she body. Dem been want fo' know if it been done right, according to the old ways." He breathed sporadically now. "And I been say yes. Yes, it been done good, according to dem damn old ways, me been say. Yes."

Meera stared at the pathetic old man, suddenly aware that she was watching death creep over him, consume him cell by cell. It was an oddly emotionless observation, one that shamed her and pushed her back into her professional demeanour. Only then did she notice that Yanni was standing behind her, his hand on her shoulder. "You heard?" she asked him.

"Yes," Yanni said. "It's a city of immigrants, you know. Everyone's got secrets and stories from some faraway place. We're supposed to start fresh when we get here, no? Let's take him back now, okay?"

But Persaud was not done yet. "Boy," he said weakly to Yanni. "Yahhhm comin' now. Go and see."

Yanni slitted his eyes in annoyance, but returned to the window nonetheless. He rushed back to report to Meera: "It's true. The fellow who was watching me is gone. I think he might have come into the hospital!"

Persaud's face contorted then. With surprising strength, he locked his hand onto Meera's arm, hurting her slightly. "Yahhhm comin'!" he gasped. Meera could sense the otherworldy terror that possessed Persaud, but could do nothing for him. She tore his grip away and began sifting through the room's supplies, searching for a sedative.

From the empty hallway came the unmistakable sound of approaching footsteps. These were not the steps of the nurses, who wore sneakers or delicate high heels, but of a heavy-set man in boots. Meera's eyes met Yanni's and the young man leapt to his feet and to the door, just in time to intercept a blond youth in a blue and white University of

Toronto jacket. "You," Yanni barked at him, "visiting hours are over. You're not supposed to be here."

"Sorry," said the youth, looking about the room sheepishly. "I'm with the student paper. I saw the light coming from the window and thought it would be a good place to get an aerial photo of the accident." He pulled a camera from his jacket pocket and showed them.

"You'll have to leave. Sorry." Yanni pushed the youth back into the hallway and towards the exit. "See?" Yanni called back to Persaud. "Not the bloody god of death!"

But, of course, Persaud had already expired. His lifeless body lay sprawled atop the bed, like a grotesque skeletal clown bedecked in striped pyjamas and pink slippers. His final expression was not that of an old man placidly accepting his final rest, nor that of a holy man content to meet his God. Rather, it was a pose of profound terror and worry, with crevices of skin radiating from his open mouth and his gaping yellowish eyes. Thankfully, Meera was not reminded of her father. He had had the good grace to slip from mortality with silent dignity, his worldly tasks completed, and with no important words left unsaid. But, she judged, not so for Manoj Persaud.

"I thought telling his story was supposed to bring him peace," Yanni said.

"He didn't tell the whole story, I think," Meera explained. "He said they brought the girl's body to him. He didn't tell us that she was still alive at the time."

Yanni slipped his hand into hers. Meera stretched up and kissed him on the cheek. "Hey," she whispered. "Midnight shift is over." ■

Chapter Two

A Memory of Flowers and Coconut

I t was the flash of scalp that caught my attention. The afternoon sun, tinted orange as its rays were squeezed between the sky and horizon, had reflected dully against the man's leathery skin, its pores winking to me in mock recognition. He had kneeled then, in obeisance to the pandit who had dabbed the red tika upon his forehead, accepting the petals of rose, jasmine and hyacinth that now littered the floor of the mandir like autumn leaves or crumpled papers upon the ground.

I had already received my blessing, had already returned to my place on the tiled and flowered floor to partake of

the closing moments of the puja ceremony, hands pious-
ly clasped together in silent reverence, a temple of flesh
formed from bony fingers and wrinkled skin. But the flash
of scalp had drawn my eyes upward. The bald man looked
to me then, as his face raised anew from the pandit's bene-
dictions, his eyes meeting mine in curious semi-recogni-
tion. I knew this man. In another life, another continent,
decades past. There had been flowers then, too.

***

"A-how dis ting happen to you foot, bhai?" The scent of
jasmine choked me, not altogether unpleasantly, cemented
into my sinuses by the pressing, familiar humidity. A man
had once told me that in the engine of our brains, the box
called "smell" had the shortest wire connecting it to the box
called "memory." The odour of jasmine, to me, was forever
linked with the memory of my mother, of all mothers, and
of women who resembled mothers.

"One drum been fall on m' foot," I told this motherlike
woman, careful not to take my attention from the task at
hand. It is difficult now, with so many years having filled
the gap of experience, literacy and education, to seamlessly
bring together the colourful Guyanese world of my mem-

ory with the present haze of halcyon dreaming. Yet, back then, we did speak in the creole of the land, that chimeric blend of English, Hindi, Dutch, French and Senegalese which characterized both the tongues and histories of the three Guyanas. When last I spoke thus, I was but a teenager unaware of the grand world beyond the fatuous vegetable markets of Georgetown and New Amsterdam, and the polished wooden boatwares of Berbice and Vreedenhoop towns. Memory of that sing-gong speech is to me bonded to recollections of a physically harder life, but a life spiced with sharp sensory delights that were made more so by the wet Caribbean heat, by the genuineness of our warm and fanciful people who seemed to feel things more potently and quixotically than do folk today, and by the blinding whiteness of the South American sun, so godlike in its tethered perch high above our menial mortal demesnes.

"You na go to one doctah?" she asked, busily daubing the "bottomhouse", the shaded underfloor of the stilted bleached domicile, with a pungent mixture of cow dung and mud.

"Yes, me been go," I said. Salim squirmed in the chair then, almost causing me to snip his ear with the scissors. "Doctah can't do nuttin'." The foot injury had no effect on my ability to walk, run or work. But it had left a gruesome scar that showed through the gaps in my rubber sandal,

like some leathery eel squirming for purchase and release
from beneath the sandal's constricting straps. It was good
for a topic of conversation, gave me something to blabber
on about while I cut someone's hair.

Salim couldn't take his eyes off my foot. I would
brusquely take his chin and force it back up so I could
focus on his crown, but his face would fall again moments
later. When he did it the third time, I smacked him lightly on the back of the head. "Sit up, bhai!" I said to him
sharply, perhaps cruelly.

"Yes, bhai, you wan' fuh look like one dem orphan
piknee?" His mother barked up at him. "Sit up, na!"

Salim sniffed back a tear and I regretted having hit him.
But it wasn't a hard hit, and he was old enough not to cry.
He was also old enough, though, to warrant a decent haircut, I should think. "Yuh see," I said, brushing some oily
snipped hairs from his shoulder, "is almost done. You like
it?" I stood him up and grinned broadly, holding for him
the hand mirror we had snatched from his older sister's
cache of toiletry items. The haircut was not a masterpiece.
After all, no boy as ugly as Salim could hope to look like
a Bombay filmi star, not with his fat jaw, weak shoulders
and rolly-polly neck. But at least he no longer resembled a
girl.

Salim took one look at himself in the hand mirror and broke into tears, running up the stairs into the house before I could oil and comb his hair properly.

"Nevah mind de bhai," his mother said, rising from her task with a huff, and wiping her hands with her apron. "He got he chores fuh do, anyhow." She reached into her ample dress pockets and dribbled a few mud-stained shillings into my palm. The clank of coin and against coin was a sweet sound akin to steel drums and full-belly humming-birds.

I stepped from the haven of bottomhouse shade into the torrent of light and heat, slinging my pack of things over my shoulder, and sauntering down the dirt road toward the canal where things would be cooler. The plan was to look for occasional work to tide me until the fishing boats left port again down the Essequibo.

As I recall that time now, it was charged paradoxically with both fretful economic desperation and a comfortable simplicity, though I suspect the latter is a function of my discontentment with modern North American life. The engines of our brains, I must remind myself, are wired to minimize the trauma of memory, to re-paint old pictures in softer tones. We recall the warmth of the sun and the joy of children, but not the ache of our empty bellies and over-taxed backs. We lazily recollect days of idle village chit-chat, but rarely hear tell of the scores of neighbours who died of curable maladies. And we cling to morphed images of sylvan bliss, yet have somehow forgotten the gaunt dirtied faces of orphaned and disabled children who sometimes watched wide-eyed from the roadside.

The memories are thus dulled, unsharpened for our own protection. Yet I know that my old Caribbean homeland conferred a vividness of perception. Back then, back there, food tasted more sharply, colours leapt at the eye, and sounds pierced the ear. The glory of rest, as it was such a rare commodity, was especially well perceived, clung to for every stretched moment.

I would rest by the canal, I decided, savouring every minute before the fishing boats recalled their crews and I was compelled to return to the jungle rivers to earn my keep. No more hair-cutting today.

These were the days before pavement, back when the cows and oxen were free to roam the avenues with impunity, at least in the Indian neighbourhoods. It was not a time of carelessness or pastoral simplicity --as much as us old people would like to remember it so. A young man not from the city would have to make his lean fortune in the cane fields, the bauxite mines or on the fishing boats. The city boys had desk jobs: clerks, officials, officers. Of course, we heard rumour of the great war in Europe, of one group of white men having attacked another group of white men, Germany having invaded France. But it had little effect on our day-to-day lives, at least for those of us in the countryside. I suppose that in the city the fuel prices were rising, and the distraught white folks in their manors were trumpeting to the newspapers their anxieties about their besieged European motherlands.

Such things could not be known to me at the time, of course. Foremost on my mind was the coolness of the breeze that would sometimes roll from the surface of the brown-water canal, a welcome though putrid breath of relief. The waters were still, used only for the transport of small boats from one river system to the next, and not for the encouragement of fish or bird life. Yet its banks were a preferred destination for the idle. The play of sunlight against the water's darkness was a delightful companion to the orchestra of odours that arose from the tufts of wildflowers, the usual parade of people and animals, and from the questionable hints of decay yards beneath the water's stillness.

I sat by the edge of the canal, letting a team of oxen trudge past me and trample the ground and ubiquitous wild flowers into an odoriferous and colourful dust cloud. There were some other young people lingering by the water: a teenaged couple trying hard to appear to be ignoring each other, their fingers occasionally brushing together shamelessly; several additional teams of oxen pulling punts of wood and produce along the canal; and another young man about my age, though with thinning hair, squatting with his eyes to the water, a cracked coconut cradled in his palms and occasionally brought to his mouth.

I found myself gaping longingly at the stream of coconut milk pouring into the young man's mouth, the sunlight reflecting off of it like one of the holy Himalayan rivers of which the pandits sometimes speak. I smacked my lips and wondered if I could afford to buy my own coconut, or whether this fellow would part with a sip or two from his own.

On the other side of the canal, at some distance, another team of oxen approached, towing a waterborne punt. This time, unless my eyes deceived me, the cargo was fruit, among them ripe coconuts and some mangoes. It was a glorious sight, one of which I never bored, though it was quite commonplace in those days. The rhythmic precision of two bonded oxen, yoked lovingly with hand-carved wooden devices, drawn by the practised hand of a child dissimilarly yoked by the unwanted chore, spoke to me of the naturalness of husbandry, of the finely tuned partnership between animals and men.

It was a scene that appealed to my Hindu blood, particularly for its employment of animals related to cows, and for its Arcadian plainness. The muscle of the oxen, the brain of a human, the wealth of the produce and the fluidity of the canal came together to transport natural goodness from one place to another, all within a colourful context flavoured by the pervading scents of the spring-time flower blooms. The small figure leading this particular team, lazily holding the reigns of the lead ox, was a distracted boy whose gaze was fixed to the sky, his fresh-cut hair the only masculine clue to his otherwise girlish demeanour. I smiled for the coincidence that had brought a sullen-faced Salim back to me.

"Salim!" I shouted at him, hoping to sweet-talk a coconut from the wretch. "Salim!" But he was too far away, his attentions focused upward into the flawless blue heavens. Following his gaze, I noticed the speck of discontinuity that seemed so inconsistent with the natural ancientness of the Caribbean sky. A zeppelin, an airship.

Twice before, in that same year, I had seen zeppelins floating north from Brazil, and had heard talk of many others. Some of the ignorant folk supposed that the ships were snatching young men to be taken to fight in the war. But that was madness. There were plenty white English soldiers for that job, plenty enough to have taken and held our mother India, they say; plenty enough to fight the Germans all by themselves, I should think.

At first, the airship was a black grain of rice held at a forearm's length, tracing a silent line from the south. In minutes, it grew to the size of two ginnip seeds, large enough to see words on its side. I could not read the words. I assumed then it was because my education was poor at the time. But I know now that I did not understand that particular language.

We watched the zeppelin turn lazily, its skin seeming to ripple against hard winds so high up. It was of a different world, another philosophy, completely and conveniently beyond my reach. I extended my hand and pretended to snatch it, to bring it down from the perfect sky. It was my wish, I suppose, to hold that token of foreignness, to imprison its metallic hide in the weaker flesh of my hand But it was too slippery, and escaped my grip, briefly occluding the sun god from my sky. Its engines were too far to be heard, but I imagined them straining to escape my fingers, dragging both me and my country across the ocean toward the war. I quickly pulled my hand back, then pretended to flick the airship from the sky with my thumb and forefinger.

Salim, too, had paused in his task to gaze heavenward in puzzlement. In his distraction, the oxen team had drawn to a halt, while the floating punt had continued forward, slamming into the side of the canal, toppling silently into the water, its heavy cargo sinking rapidly toward the bottom.

"Salim!" I shouted at him. "Loose dem ox! Cut line!" The young man with the thinning hair leapt to his feet and dropped his coconut, startled by this development. The halved coconut rolled toward me, assailing my nostrils with that delicious smell of sweet goodness. But my thoughts were no longer of quenching my thirst. Salim either could not hear me, or was paralysed by fright. Had he cut the ropes then, had freed the oxen, the horror that ensued would have been avoided.

The ropes connecting the animals to the sinking punt took up their slack and strained taught. The lagging ox grunted loudly as its footing began to fail, its head being pulled down toward the canal's water. In seconds, its forelegs were in the water, its body sliding along the wet bank. Moments later, with a sickening *glub-glub* noise, both oxen were in the water, spiralling in orbit about an invisible centre beneath which the heavy punt was still sinking.

It was too late to do anything, we all knew. To swim out to the beasts, to cut them free, would welcome personal drowning. The heavy sinking animals would suck us under the water. This was especially true for me and my bad foot. The three of us –I, Salim and the coconut man– stood there on the banks, wide-eyed and stupefied, as the oxen wailed that terrible sound. One of the beasts submerged with little fight, its neck broken by the yoke's torque. The other was pulled into a slow, agonizing drowning death, its caterwauls scratching against our eardrums, approaching a shrill tonality unheard of from animals as large and as powerful as these. His face was too distant for me to see clearly, but I imagined that Salim's tears flowed in torrents.----

Today, Salim's is a casual parlour tale I tell in modern comfort. But it had no doubt been a life-changing catastrophe for him and his family. The boy's fate is unknown to me, as I had soon tired of the scene and continued my trek to the docks where the fishing boats were collecting new workers. Decades have filled the chasm between that memorable day and the present; the years having been busied with emigrations, maturation, education and a failing battle against old age.

As certain floral scents take me to pleasant times of maternal bliss and village congeniality, so the smell and taste of coconut milk and trampled wildflowers draw me to that afternoon by the muddy canal, when a potent image of my country's rural life was supplanted and destroyed by the intrusion of a foreign machine. That I would, in later years, be carried by such machines to alien lands where my way of speech, my sense of humour, my understanding of history and of the natural world would be massaged and re-formed, brings me a certain thoughtfulness akin to sadness. Memories of anger or despair, if they were ever felt, have long since been buried beneath the years, untethered from the record for their foreignness against the sylvan temperance of my motherland.

That is why, when I recognized the coconut man so many years later at a puja in Toronto, his thinning hair replaced with a leathery bald scalp that caused me to squint in its reflected brightness, I neither cried nor reared in surprise, but simply smiled knowingly, warmed by a welcome link to a past long lost. ■

Chapter Three

Destroyer of Worlds

In a dream, I sit in the Clarchen Ballhaus in Berlin on ladies' night, waiting for Marlene Dietrich to slither across the dance floor, deposit herself onto my welcoming lap, tip back her top-hat, and spew a luminous funnel of unfiltered cigarette smoke from her painted lips.

In another, I am written into an adolescent science-fiction novel by Robert Heinlein, destined to fall into the arms of a domineering small-town teenage girl before I am shipped off on a rocket mission to re-conquer Venus.

In others, I am loveless and barren, forsaken and forlorn.

"I had two dreams about you this week," Tanya says. My ears prick up, more alert than any time since a past lover's husband had unpredictably entered the apartment. "In the first dream," she continues, "we were having a coffee, then you kissed me. I had to stop you because, you know, I have a boyfriend."

"And in the second?"

"In the second dream, I didn't stop you."

"And how was I?" Her eyelids flutter and she giggles in that nasty fake baritone that only women can master. And that's where it had to end. After she's had me in a dream, how can I, a real man who doesn't go away with the dawn, compare? No ego, my friend, is that secure.

I had two dreams about Ariadne this past week. In the first, I'm in the airport parking lot. I look up and see her frowning down at me from a Calvin Klein billboard; she was goddess-like in her stature and radiance. In the second dream, she and I switch bodies and begin to dance. I think it was the samba. But instead of exploring our new anatomy, all we were concerned about was who got to lead.

Illogic is the mantra of the dream state, chaos its mode and tack. Yet order springs from the jumble, a story percolates and the ego imposes a relevance often mistaken for spirituality.

In the tradition of my people, the god Vishnu sleeps at the centre of the world, dreaming the universe, causing its being. From his navel grows a lotus, and on that lotus sits the quantum-mechanical god Brahma. Brahma opens his eyes and a world comes into existence. He closes his eyes and a world vanishes from existence. If Vishnu were to shift his colossal body in sleep, disturbing Brahma in his wakefulness, perhaps the lotus-sitter would blink, and all would be naught.

I am a destroyer of worlds, a divine egoist, the ultimate mood killer. A thousand lives blink into being with the start of my unconscious cinema, and a thousand more are quietly extinguished as I slip back into wakefulness. I am a creator of worlds, ephemeral and transient, wherein thin lives shimmer and etiolate, servicing my will yet tormenting my id.

To have dreamt a world is to have willed new life from the blackness. Contemplations on the origins of life usually begin with the accidents of electrochemistry and the violent swirling of sweet primordial soup, thick as Indian dahl, that spits forth blobs of organic goop. From this follows the accidental collisions of simple molecules into organic strings, eventually into amino and nucleic acids, and from there to the stirring of unconscious life.

Sometimes I wonder if we are indeed organic machines that have developed the magic of consciousness, or if we are instead pure intellect that has learned to express itself in the physical world. Perhaps there exists a vast field of intelligence, pan-dimensional and incomprehensible, that

pops and percolates, occasionally protruding and project-
ing into the thin and inconsequential plane of physical existence. Is there, then, intelligence in every atom, a shadow
of a soul haunting every quark and neutrino? If so, then
we are indeed the dream, existing at the pleasure of the
dreamer. All matter becomes but a state of awareness.

But these are distractions and rationalizations, paths
into the darkness of intellect, away from the light of mind-
less beauty, that realm of intended quantum restfulness.

I dreamed once of plains of perfection, on which all
failed loves repaired and rejoiced. Therein lies the power of
that world, its lesson to be transported to the wakeful. Its
events are plastic and nonsensical, transcending logic and
reason. Yet its feel is contentment, proving that satisfaction
can issue from formless irrationality. To stray from the
intellect is indeed bliss.

"Tomorrow is Tuesday," Sneha whispers to me seduc-
tively through the soma ether, and I howl in laughter, as
if it is the funniest joke I've ever heard. There is no sense
in dream-time, no reason for sadness, humour, anger or
titillation. Emotions erupt from the id without first being
summoned; there are no rules. It is a quantum mechan-
ical thing, wherein effect can comfortably precede cause,
laughter precede the joke, and love precede acquaintance-
ship.

Thus is the comfort of Vishnu and Brahma. They are the sleeping and sleepwalking gods, icons to the weird set of quantum formulae. Our world, their dream, is stoked by the irrational, spiced with the unpredictable and pricked by the nonsensical.

In a dream, I lie next to my beloved, ecstatic in halcyon slumber. Her breath sings in time with my own, the cadence reaching beneath the conscious to the next dream, then below that to the dream of the fundament. Ours is an orchestra of sleep, bound in rhythm to the dance of the quantum gods, and played with love and tranquility.

My beloved arises and rubs the sleep from her eyes. She thinks to herself, "I am a destroyer of worlds, a divine egoist, the ultimate mood killer." ■

Chapter Four

My Girlfriend's Tattoo

O kay, here's the story.

The girlfriend, she's always had this fascination with half moons. Not just any half moons, but that cute gothic half moon with the pointy nose and perverse smile --the one you see a lot of in MacDonald's commercials. Sure, there's a literary precedent for this: the Man in the Moon, pre-Verne science-fiction, sentimentalist visual art, that sort of thing. But it can still be an annoying obsession.

Above her bed dangles a roughly-fashioned pointy-nosed half moon "man" made of gold-covered cardboard, suspended star-like by a silvery gossamer thread. Around her neck often hangs a gold half moon pendant, its slick smile appealing morbidly to my heightened sense of protectionist jealousy. And even I, caught up in romance and rare generosity, had purchased for her a half moon belt buckle from the seedy bazaars of Bangkok.

But for months her obsession had taken another form: a desire to imprint the lasting half moon legacy on her sweet body forever more, in tattoo form.

Ecch!

The thought horrified me. Images of scabby unhygienic intrusions into her unmarked white flesh were troublesome to me. I pleaded: it's unclean! It'll fade! It's *gross*! It'll hurt!

For weeks she soothed me with sweet salvos: It'll be small; it'll be a tiny thing on my hip; it'll never see sunlight; only *you* will ever see it.

Appeals to my neanderthal ways of sexual exclusivity are always effective. That last bit was sufficient to quell my desperate vocal objections. Still, fortunately for me, she is an endless procrastinator. I knew it would take her months to realize her plan.

Well, months passed. And with each day her plan took on greater substance. She chose the colours, the design and the perpetrator. I sighed. What could I do?

Then I began to think. Well, thought I, it's actually kind of sexy. Especially considering its location south of the panty line. Gradually, as carnal stirrings gained energy beneath my vocal chords, I came to salivate at the prospect of a more careful and personal examination of the tattoo when it finally arrived. I would never admit such a thing to her, of course, but in such matters my spinal cord takes high precedence over my moral cerebrum.

And, of course, days before the eager event was to take place, she dumped me. ■

Chapter Five

New

He coughed and wiped his mouth with his sleeve, then looked up at his parents with broad, baleful eyes. Shiny and brown –almost cartoonish– they probed for reassurance and meaning, but found only loving concern.

"This is ridiculous, Brenda." Jose stooped to tie his son's shoes, yanking on the loops so tightly that his knuckles turned white. Alejandro's only response was to deepen his unblinking stare. "We really so desperate now?"

With tired hands, a mother's wistful affection swept over Alejandro, feeling his moist scalp and thinning brown hair. The boy shivered to the touch and turned his sweet head to meet Brenda's warm hand. "We try everything," she said. "Everything. Understand?"

Jose shrugged and hoisted his son onto his shoulders, summoning a semblance of light joy as he marched his small family into their rusting station wagon. They drove in silence, with Alejandro's head pressed into Brenda's bosom, while his large eyes darted across the rapidly passing panorama, absorbing as much of the visual information as his growing brain could process.

They arrived at the prescribed address, an unassuming single-story bungalow in the suburbs of the cool Canadian city. In front, loud multiracial children played ball hockey and ran thoughtlessly across lawns and driveways, though none seemed either inclined or sufficiently brave to trespass past the whipping, tattered red flags that ringed the exterior of this particular house.

Fingers intertwined in nervous hope, a thumb pressed against a chipped door buzzer, and a small brown youth opened the door. A practiced grin spread across the youth's face, and all eyes were drawn to his shaven head and poorly fitted spectacles. "Welcome," he said, pressing the palms of his hands together, then wiping them on his flannel shirt before offering one to Jose. "My name is Manish. Come, come." He beckoned them into a sitting room with no seats, only cushions on the floor, and backed away, saying, "Guru-*ji* will see you in a moment."

Jose slitted his eyes and shook his head at Brenda. Above her head, a cheap poster on the wall declared the unending and absolute wisdom embodied by the Hindu deity

Ganesh, god of learning. On the opposite wall hung a magnificent black and gold poster of a long-haired young man in short pants, grimacing in either pain or anger. Across his chest blazed the words, "ACDC World Tour, 1985."

"This is a waste!" Jose finally said aloud. He did not notice that Manish had returned with a tray of sweet tea for his guests.

"Why do you say that?" Manish asked without looking up, serving the tea to both adults, before contemplating Alejandro's bright-eyed detachment and denying him a cup. "Guru-*ji* does not charge a fee. So, this visit costs you nothing. And today is a Sunday, not a work day. You've wasted neither time nor money by coming here."

"Unless he has somewhere else to be," said a steady feminine voice emanating from behind Manish. "Then this visit takes him from that place."

Manish bowed and backed away from his guru's path, allowing her entry into the room. Her appearance did not quell Jose's concerns. She was an Indian woman in her mid-forties, extremely thin and slight, with her oily black hair tied uncomfortably tightly in a bun. Like Manish, her bony face was adorned with cheap, wiry spectacles, as if their shared ascetic lifestyle had rendered them both nearsighted. But what shocked Jose the most was

Guru-*ji*'s most un-guru-like attire. Instead of the pristine, hand-wrought cotton robes he had expected, this young woman was at the apex of modern suburban slacker chic, with unwashed jogging shorts, dollar-store flip-flops and a faded pink Breast Cancer Awareness t-shirt.

Brenda sprang to her feet and mimicked Manish's namaste and pressed palm greeting. "Thank you for seeing us... Guru-*ji*", she said, averting her eyes from the guru's.

"Call me Latika," The brown woman sang, her lilting voice effortless melodic and light. "Don't be like that simpering Manish. Look me in the eye, Brenda. I'm not your mother or your teacher."

Brenda blushed, but Jose grunted. "When do we start?" he asked.

"We've started," Latika said. "Sit and drink your tea." She sunk into a cross-legged position with the couple, waving away Manish. She waited for almost a minute in silence, smiling at her guests, before holding out a hand to Alejandro.

"Go," Brenda whispered into her son's ear, and pushed him forward. Latika caught his faulty lurch and let him slip into her lap, his head turned to look her in the eye.

"He looks like he's only two, but he's actually almost seven--"

"Shh, Brenda," Latika interrupted her.

With an almost plant-like litheness, Latika held the child lightly within the cage of her bony arms, bobbing rhythmically and unconsciously, as would any woman reflexively when cradling a baby. She sniffed his scalp and seemed to examine the crown of his head, then uncurled the boy's tiny hands to rub his soft palms with her long thumbs. Throughout it all, she maintained a crooked, toothy grin, and hummed –almost imperceptibly – a dancing tune that hinted at distant familiarity.

"He does not talk?" Latika asked, holding Alejandro up to her face and staring into his unblinking eyes.

"No," Brenda replied. "But he does understand us. He does what he's told."

"Does he sing?" Latika asked.

"Sing?" Jose interrupted. "She just told you he doesn't make a noise!"

Latika giggled under her breath. "Brenda said he doesn't talk. But I think he can make noises. Can't you, boy?"

"His name is Alejandro," Jose corrected.

"Indeed," Latika confirmed. "Sneha told me about him. About all of you. She works with you, Brenda, right? She's the one who gave you my name?" Brenda nodded aggressively, leaning forward hopefully. "His name is Alejandro. I will remember that."

Latika broke out into a big grin, licked her lips, then sang nonsense notes to accompany the strange tune she had been humming, "La-go-da-mum-go-rah-tah-tee-sam-naaaa." To the amazement of all, Alejandro broke into a broad babyish smile and gurgled the same tune from somewhere deep in his throat.

Brenda gasped and lunged to her feet. Jose clutched her hand she cried out, "My God! How did you do that?!"

"I did nothing," Latika said calmly, barely looking Brenda in the eye. "Alejandro did it. He could always do it." She lifted her arms and Alejandro instantly sprang to his feet and ran back to his mother's embrace.

"Do it again, baby," Brenda implored him, clutching his face as she would a precious gem. "Sing for mommy." But Alejandro just stared at her in his unblinking, probing way. "Why won't he sing for me? I'm his mother!"

But Latika's only response was a subtle head bob, simultaneously suggesting sagacity, ignorance and melancholy. Instead of answering, she asked more questions. "You've taken him to a doctor, yes?"

"Yes, many," Brenda answered. "They say there's nothing biologically wrong with him. He ages very very slowly. And they don't think he's autistic. He passes every test they know how to give. They even scanned his brain and found nothing wrong. But clearly there's something wrong!"

"There are many more specialists we can see," Jose added. "But Brenda felt we should see someone more.... natural."

Latika blinked in a long, tired way, then took a soothing sip from her tea. "There's nothing unnatural about doctors," she finally said. "What are doctors but men and women, products of nature? We are all natural, and all that we create is natural. The machine that the doctors used to scan your son's head was made from metals mined from the Earth, all natural things. The medicines they give you are extracted from natural plants. All that is manmade is in fact nature-made, since Man is himself made by nature."

Jose frowned. "You know what I mean," he said angrily. "All that crystal, vegetarian and sandal-wearing... stuff."

"I'm sorry, Latika!" Brenda's face turned a deep red. "Jose is just frustrated. We're both grateful for your time. Really."

Jose grunted. "Don't apologize for me. The doctors, nutritionists and psychiatrists --they all said they could help, too. I accept no one at face value anymore."

Latika smiled and lowered her eyes. "I never said I could help," she said. Brenda's spirits fell visibly, and even Jose was silenced. "I fear that Alejandro's ...condition... is not a physical, psychological or even spiritual one. I think it's elemental." Jose made a peculiar face, as if he had smelled something foul. Before he could say anything, though, Latika beckoned them to stand and to follow her to the rear of the house. They acquiesced, but Jose grumbled noticeably.

She led them through a cheap wall of beads that clamoured with their passing, creating a noise akin to water rushing through a brook. From that point on, Brenda thought that she could hear strange music distantly in the recesses of her awareness. The style of music was alien to her. It was neither vocal nor instrumental, reminiscent of no cultural tradition with which she was familiar; but it was unmistakably music, with tonalities set to a cadence and separated by tonal and pitch spaces that reverberated within her, suggesting that it was something more than noise.

"Do you hear that?" She asked. "The music?"

"I hear whispers," Jose said. "Sounds like the old Jewish men arguing over morning coffee in the shop downstairs from us, no?"

"I hear nothing," Latika said. "But I'm not listening right now. Or maybe I'm going deaf." She forced a strange, polite and awkward laugh, as would someone unaccustomed to regular social contact. Alejandro gazed up at her, expressionless.

Latika gestured to the floor. It was then that Brenda and Jose noticed that they were in the bungalow's renovated rear kitchen. All the appliances had been removed, but the orientation of the room was unmistakable. The windows had been boarded up and upon the counters were a series of hand-carved granite statues situated in a haphazard and unaesthetic fashion. A few were depictions of deities from various cultures around the world. Brenda and Jose recognized the elephant-headed Hindu god Ganesh again, as well as a couple of frightening images from the Afro-Caribbean tradition of Santoria, and the famous icon of the Egyptian god Anubis. But most of the statues were portrayals of everyday human existence: a man carrying a basin of water on his shoulder, a woman brushing her long hair, a child tying his shoes.

On the hardwood floor, where Latika bade them look, was a spot of light created by a directed fluorescent bulb on the ceiling. Latika selected a statue from the counter and placed it in the light.

"This is Shiva," she said.

It was a famous image, that of a multi-armed, feminine man poised in mid-dance, clutching both a drum and a torch, and standing upon what appeared to be a demonic little dwarf, all wrapped by a fiery halo that encircled the entire scene. "This is Shiva's manifestation as Nataraj, the Lord of the Dance. He creates life with the drum and removes life with the flame. The end and the beginning are always the same, guided by the same principles, which here are represented by a god, which, you must understand, is only an artistic choice. The essence of the image is that the seeds of the finale are always planted at the opening. And there is always a return, a rebirth. We are all tied to the great wheel of happenings and happenstance."

"You're talking about reincarnation," Jose said. There was no judgement in his voice, no emotion at all, really. It was merely a statement of fact. But with Jose, there was always a suggestion of discontentment. "You're going to tell us about our son's past lives."

"No," Latika said, but offered no explanation. She reached down and adjusted the statue, fluidly gesturing to the creature beneath the god's foot. "See at his feet? The priests have their own ideas about the thing on which Nataraj stands. But I will tell you what I see. It is what you Christians call the Beast."

Brenda gasped. But Jose protested: "We aren't Christians. We have no religion." Latika acquiesced with a smile and bobbled her head slightly.

"The Beast --you mean it's the devil?"

"No, Brenda. I don't think that there's a personage of evil. There is no devil, at least not in my perception. Surely, there are things that mean each of us harm. But the Beast, it is more of an... imperfection. It is an error in the system, a mote in the divine eye. Nataraj seeks to suppress the error, the contamination, before the next cycle of rebirth; but he cannot contain all of it. Thus, the world is always poisoned anew. Thus, each of us is less than the perfect child that is expected by whatever gods you believe in. In the mindset of the West, it is the Beast that makes us human. But it is also the Beast that locks us to the cycle of rebirth, as we strive for the perfection that can never arise."

Jose reached for his son and held him tightly. Alejandro submitted to the embrace but did not return it. As always, his eyes were locked to Latika's face, exploring each minute blemish and pock mark, seeming to memorize every shade and contour. "And what does this have to do with Alejandro? Are you saying he's got no Beast? That he's –I don't know – perfect?"

Latika laughed. "Not at all! I'm sorry, but your son is as far from perfect as any of us. His flaws are evident, no? I'm sorry for being so blunt, but it's my way. No, I tell you all this because I want you to understand what I do."

"And what is it that you do, O great guru," Jose demanded, dripping with rude sarcasm, "Other than play with statues and build your mystique?" Brenda shot him a nasty look.

"Ah," Latika said, sidestepping Jose's confrontational tone. "This is where it gets difficult. I don't have the right words to describe exactly what I do. I've tried many times. I've had others try, too, like Manish. Somehow it always comes out sounding like metaphysical hippy nonsense, especially when Manish tries! You know what I mean, right, Jose?"

"Try anyway," he said.

"I commune with the Beast," Latika said. She waited for the gravity of her words to set in, then sat cross-legged across from the statue of Nataraj. She motioned for the others to sit, as well. Surprisingly, Alejandro was the first to comply.

Latika cocked her head, as if summoning her focus, then smiled coyly. "I hear it now," she said, then briefly hummed a queer little tune barely beneath her breath. "Okay, listen to me," She sat up straight and cleared her face of all expression. "It's the imperfection that defines us, that tells the tale of our journey. How can you tell a photocopy from the original? By the slight error that was made in copying, because no reproduction is perfect. The journey of the information from the source document to the photocopy is characterized by the error that was made in copying.

Maybe that error is a blurring, maybe a blemish. But now the information has something new to it. The error is the new thing."

Jose rubbed his eyes in a dramatic, fatiguing display.

"Stay with me, Jose," Latika said. "The error is information. The Beast is information. If you can recognize the Beast within each of us, you can read the book of that person's journey. And I think you know what journey I'm talking about."

Jose sighed. "Again, it's reincarnation, right?" Brenda leaned forward excitedly.

"It's a limiting word," Latika explained. "There are cycles of life within a life and between lives and even external to life. All matter is energy —Einstein showed us that — and all energy is information. Everything in creation is information. We are, each of us, made of the same types of atoms and molecules and energies as everyone else. It's the way those things are put together that constitute what we perceive to be our individuality. That's just information, in a real, physical sense."

Brenda nodded, but Jose continued to project impatience.

"I will suggest to you that the essence of a living thing is more complicated than just the assembly of our parts or the extent of our information, or even the sum total of our experiences, though all those things play a role. Do not forget, as well, that as biological living things we are each in essence a colony of lifeforms, of independent cells working together to produce the illusion of biological individuality. A single blood cell or muscle cell is a life unto itself. You begin to sense, I hope, how much of the truth of your being is hidden behind convenient illusions."

Latika searched her guests' faces for signs of comprehension. She wasn't sure she saw it, but kept going nonetheless: "But beyond all this, and indeed including all of this, is what I will call the subtle identity that mutates as it ages and grows. The subtle identity is a smidgen pinched from the hide of reality –of God, if that makes you feel better. Because of this essential, elemental link to the divinity of the universe's origins, we are all, every one of us, as old as Creation itself. We are organs of the universe." She paused, then: "I'm sorry if this appears to conflict with your Christian beliefs..."

"I told you," Jose interrupted. "We aren't religious."

"So you said," Latika agreed, bowing her head slightly. "Please forgive my stubborn ways."

Brenda threw up her hands. "Latika, I'm very open minded, and I came here with great hopes. But I still don't see what any of this has to do with my son."

Latika held up her hand in a gesture of obeisance and nodded. "Okay, okay. Listen. All of this is my way of saying that I do not hold with much of what you have probably read about reincarnation or the transmigration of souls. All that nonsense bubbles so readily through both of our cultures now that much of it has ceased to make any sense. But I use the word 'soul' while I simultaneously curse our limited human language for not giving me a better term to use. So we will speak of souls and of rebirths and the personal legacy of each of us that reaches back –far back!–– to the very moments of Creation. And my gift..." Latika took a moment to sigh. "My gift is the ability to see –through very blurry glasses, mind you!–– the length of that legacy. The dimension of time is collapsed in my eye, and I see the path of souls from imperfection to imperfection. The Beast is my guide, so to speak."

Brenda's gaze was quizzical. Jose, on the other hand, had the subtle posture of a fighter, though Latika sensed a different sentiment lingering in his mind: horror.

"So here it is," Latika said, claiming the moment. "Here is my gift in action." She locked her eyes onto Jose's face, absorbing its every crack, line, nuance and tremor. "You, Jose, have been down this path many times before. You've been a healer, a labourer, a leader and more. With each turn of the great wheel, chance has lain before you an opportunity to glimpse the gears of universal truth, as it does today. At each turn, though, you have balked. Maybe it's fear, maybe it's pride, maybe it's something else. I don't know why, but you've always balked. Insight has always been within your reach, though strangely unpleasant to your touch." Jose snarled, but said nothing.

Latika's body was as still as one of her statues, but her head swivelled to rest her eyes' piercing gaze on Alejandro's mother. She lingered there for a few heartbeats before pronouncing her findings. "And you, Brenda, have always held love lightly in your palms, have always cherished it. But often you've lost it. And the fear of further loss has since held sway at the core of your personality." Brenda smiled sweetly, and her eyes moistened somewhat. "Yours is an all too common pain, I'm afraid."

"And I..." Latika continued. "Well, my history is irrelevant. What is important here is to realize how much of this has happened before. Each of us has tread a similar path, housed in different shells, at previous points in time. All of this is well worn, all of it except..."

"Alejandro!" Brenda touched her face and considered her silent son with new fascination.

The boy coughed into the nook of his elbow, as his mother had taught him to do, then wiped his reddening eyes. His silence had never been perceived by his mother as lack of intelligence, but rather as a kind of precocious sagacity. He would speak when he had something to say, Brenda had often said, though it was clear that she feared otherwise.

Jose, on the other hand, suspected a more dire prognosis, that his son suffered from an as yet unrecognized form of mental and physical retardation. Alejandro would never speak, Jose feared; he would never tell his parents that he loved them, would never yell in joy and anger at fellow children in the schoolyard, would never coo sweet tidings into the ears of suitors, and would never engage in the rich, warm fabric of human culture that carries the rest of us from infanthood to old age. All such paths of demonstrable humanity were dependent upon the intimate and profound communication between individuals, whether vocal or subtle; the boy would be denied entry into such essential networks of human interconnectedness. Alejandro, Jose feared, was half a person, destined for a life of bare sustenance without meat and sweetness.

And what a short life it would be, for daily the boy developed new physical ailments. At first it had been the standard bugaboos of childhood: colds, diarrhea and frequent malaise. But as those refused to go away, they were joined by physical weakness, sleeplessness, random pains, multiple allergies and emotional disengagement. Throughout it all, though –even during the malaise––Alejandro maintained his gaze of fascination. All things in his world were scrutinized by his large, oval eyes. Yes, he did blink, but somehow no one ever seemed to notice when he did. He appeared to all as an intense dwarfish statue. A voyage into his eye, through the backs of his retinas and along his blazing optic nerves into the recesses of his little head, would find a brain in constant change, perpetually rewiring itself into billions of new configurations.

As a wilting, crooked and staid statue he might appear; but in all the universe, perhaps there was no other being in greater flux.

"Look at him, at his beautiful eyes," Latika implored. "Don't look at Alejandro with your eyes, though, but with your hearts; not with love, but with your subtle senses. Do you see the strangeness? He is apart, disconnected. Do you see?"

At this, Brenda burst into tears. "What do you mean?!" she demanded. "My son is beautiful and perfect. But he's sick. I need you to tell me what's wrong with him so I can make him better. I don't need you to tell me he's strange! Everyone tells me he's strange! Tell me something new!"

Alejandro dislodged his gaze from Latika's bony face and turned to consider his weeping mother. His expression was one of curiosity. It seemed to intensify his pallor. Jose reached out and took his woman's hand. "Brenda, that's exactly what she's telling us: something new."

At that, Latika smiled. "Ahhh, Jose! You are getting it! So many times at the brink of knowledge, and now you've begun to shuffle closer to the edge! Listen: the thing that I've called the Beast, in Alejandro it is tiny and pristine, so very new. There is no hint of ancientness within your son, no copying errors, so to speak, no information about his journey, the transmigrations of his subtle identity. In all the worlds in all the universe –in all the versions of the universe-- your son is unique. He is the only new thing, the only one of us who was not here at Creation. He is apart from the essential, a genuine alien in the most profound sense of the word."

"He is..." Jose stammered, considering his son anew, with a gaze coloured with love, sadness, resignation and awe, "He is... invisible to God." The theatre implicit in his words surpised even him, but their weight seemed appropriate. Latika lowered her eyes, and Brenda wept.

The sun had risen that morning promptly at 5:45 AM. By coincidence, both Manish and Jose had been standing at their front doors at that very moment: Manish engaged in his morning prayers, Jose collecting the Sunday newspaper. Both had looked up to note the emergence of the gargantuan ball of nuclear fire above the Earthly horizon, and each had considered its singular truth through different lenses. For Manish, the daybreak event was the daily reaffirmation of Heaven's covenant with the Earth, that life would spring anew with the passing of the unavoidable darkness. For Jose, it was a marker of time, a heralding of the day to come, and a reminder of the diminishing days ahead.

Unknown to both, Alejandro had also watched the sunrise. Suffering yet another sleepless night, he had perched by his bedroom window and had noted the passage of black to light. Yet he saw no difference between the two. Light and dark, day and night, energy and entropy, presence and absence: in an essentialist reduction, all were indistinguishable, differentiated solely by an arbitrary definition of states. The observation hinted at a deeper possibility, one that his barely conscious child's mind could not consider, but nonetheless felt, that delineations between existence and non-existence were equally as superfluous and arbitrary. He came to appreciate the possibility that all was illusory, a dream state without a dreamer. And again, his brain had slipped into flux.

The questions of profound singular existence that mark the maturity of a man would not ever occur to Alejandro. He would never seek a guru or father from whom to wrest the supposed secrets of the universe. The plaguing obsessions of the sentient human animal, the questions of meaning and purpose, would not beset young Alejandro, who would see such predilections as circular curiosities, pointless given that that what passed for essential truths were self-evident to any who cared to perceive them. The most fundamental of these truths could not, in any case, be expressed within the maddening constraints of limited human language. Rather it would need to be appreciated by the fullness of being, both temporal and subtle, eventually percolating to the surface of consciousness with a dismissive expression of nihilism: that it doesn't really matter.

"God has forsaken our child?" Brenda cried, surprising herself with her own dramatic choice of words, stirred perhaps by Jose's own invoking of the godhead.

"I thought you weren't religious?" Latika teased. "I don't know, Brenda. I don't know if there is a God or many gods. And if there is, I don't know what is in his –or her, or their–– heart. I can only tell you what I know, and it is this: to the extent that my gift permits, I perceive that Alejandro is the first and only true, genuine child to be birthed in Creation. The only question that perplexes me is who, then, birthed him?"

Brenda fumed in misdirected emotion. "I birthed him!" she exclaimed. "I'm his mother!"

"No, Brenda," Latika said calmly. "Remember, being blunt is my way. Yes, he emerged from your body. His body is the child of both your bodies. That is why he looks like you, and probably has some minor mannerisms in common with you. But none of us is, in essence, the product of our parents. We are each pinched from the nascent godhead, and handed down through the ages from womb to womb." She sensed Brenda's growing anger, and hastened to add, "This in no way minimizes your maternal rights or realities. He suckled at your teats and calls you mother!"

Latika regretted the last, for she knew that Alejandro would never call Brenda anything, least of all mother.

"No," Jose said coolly. "There are other questions. Why is he sick, and how do we make him well?"

Latika stood and began to walk around the former kitchen, pausing to caress certain statues. She lingered at one depicting an Asian toddler clinging to a squirming, live fish. "In a sense, all children are new," she said. "Their flesh is unsoiled, their minds, to some extent, blank slates. But, as we've discussed, each of us ancient. The newness of this girl child, amazed by the simple thrashing of a fish, is not so remarkable, as charming as we might find it."

She sat down again and adjusted her hair bun. "Now all of this sounds quite airy fairy to you, I'm sure; especially you, Jose." Alejandro's father smirked. "But you will be surprised to know that only at this point do I enter the realm of speculation. I have no evidence or strong feeling for what I'm about to tell you, only suspicion. It is this: Alejandro is new, foreign to the universe, unknown to it..."

Jose interrupted: "Are you saying that the universe is rejecting him, like a disease or an allergy?" Brenda glared at the father of her child in horror.

"No, Jose," Latika said. "But I appreciate that your mind is opening to possibilities. The universe is not an organism with an immune system and enemies to repel; it is not rejecting Alejandro. It is, for lack of a better word, consuming him."

Latika's words were met with silence, something she did not expect. She looked straight at Brenda and raised her eyebrows, hoping to elicit a comment. "But his body grows," Brenda finally said. "It grows slowly, but it grows. Nothing is consuming him! And why would God, or the universe, choose to do this?"

"It's a poor word, 'consume,'" Latika sighed, once more taking note of Brenda's use of theological language. "Let me put it this way: not only is Alejandro the first and only true child to be born in the universe, he will also be the first and only being to truly die. He will not be reborn, in any facet or sense, except that his constituent atoms will return to the material world. Unlike the rest of us, whose subtle identities continue the journey with the universe, Alejandro will desist."

Latika looked then to Jose, to see if his opening mind would take the next step with her. But he was silent. "Have you ever wondered why we die?" Latika asked in an annoying professorial tone. She did not wait for an answer. "There are some who believe that the universe itself is finite. It is hurtling towards its own demise. To understand its own death, it lives mortal lives through each of us. But as we are each universal flesh, we don't truly perish."

Unexpectedly, Jose broke out into a wide grin. "The ancient myths," he grunted. "Greek tales and the lot. It's the mortals who are the heroes and the gods who are jealous." Again, Brenda glared at Jose, the turmoil of emotions evident behind her expression.

"Right!" Latika exclaimed. "Mortality provides insight into meaning. something the immortals crave. Alejandro--" She caught herself about to weep, and the thrush of emotion lodged in her throat. This was so unlike her, to be overcome in the heat of her work. "Alejandro is an unforeseen opportunity to experience true death. He is a universe unto himself."

Brenda sniffed, wiped her eyes on her sleeve and pushed herself to her feet. She reached down and snatched Alejandro's arm; he did not resist, but did not disengage his fascination for Latika's face. "Come on, Jose. We're leaving. Plenty of real doctors left to see." She marched her son towards the front of the house and out the front door, pushing past a beaming Manish in the process.

Jose stood slowly, taking the time to straighten his clothes. Latika watched him wordlessly, waiting for him to speak. Finally: "So what do we do? Help us, please."

"I don't know," Latika confessed, her arms held wide. "This is all quite beyond me. But I will tell you what I feel. Today is Sunday and you are guilty that you are not in your Christian church." She sensed Jose's impending objection and held up a hand to silence him. "Go to your church and pray for your son. It's as good as anything else you can do. The thing about gods is that they're allowed to break the rules. They're the only ones, I should think."

Jose considered her, tight-lipped, then turned to follow his family into their car. Latika sidled up alongside Manish outside the front door to watch them drive off.

"I don't hear the music anymore," Manish said, pressing his hands to his ears and swaying theatrically. "I was quite enjoying the tune."

"Me neither. I've lost it, too," Latika said. "It was quite something, yes? To hear the the gears of Heaven, or the songs of eternity. Whatever it was. I think that boy allowed us to hear the strings of Creation strummed by an excited god. I'm running out of colourful metaphors, Manish. Do remember to elbow me the next time I go on about energies and gods and such things." They both enjoyed a little laugh, but there was no mistaking the taint of melancholy within their exchange.

In the car, Alejandro's head was turned to keep an unblinking eye on Latika's receding face. After some seconds, she could no longer be seen, but Alejandro continued to stare in her direction. It had been many hours since he had ceased perceiving the shells of reality, freed now to consider the empty spaces between atoms, the true meat of the world. Matter, in his eye, was only the organization of energy as simple arithmetic progressions. And time was an orthogonal projection on a mathematical plane, nothing more. But in Latika's face he had found the one thing that gave him understanding of self: a reflection, a mirror.

But no more. He turned to sit comfortably in the back of the car, no longer able to focus on the sounds, smells, touches and sights of this world. It was all drowned out now by the deafening elemental music that resonated with his every atom. For this is what he would be now and forevermore: a divine song, fading and spread eternally across the cosmic winds. □

Chapter Six

Besting Death

"Who is that man, Jai?"

"Which man, Gaitri?"

"The one over there talking to my sister Anita. The tall man, the one with the old-fashioned hat and grey kurta."

"Oh. Isn't that Nikhil, the boy Anita's marrying?" Jai started digging in the sandbox. Apparently, he'd lost something in the sand. "Can you help me find my marbles?"

"Later, Jai. I'm going to find out who that man is."

"Don't go, Gaitri! If he's not Nikhil, then it's not your business. It's a grown-up thing, na? And I need you to help me find my lost marbles!" He tugged at Gaitri's sleeve. She was only a few months older, but Jai relied on her as he would an adult.

"Later," Gaitri said, and walked to the picnic table where Anita and the strange man were talking. His posture and form were somewhat familiar, but Gaitri knew he was a stranger. Anita appeared to know him quite well, however.

"The world is grey," the man was saying to Gaitri's sister. "We perceive colour where there is only shade, and polarity where there is nuance. We do this –*you* do this—to quell the pain, to make the unbearable bearable. But your choices do not change the truth of things, that there is only grey."

"You are a strange one, Uncle," Anita replied, giggling in way that bordered on condescension. "Why tell me these things? What am I to do with such knowledge?"

The man frowned then sighed. "I am not certain why I take the time, child. But I know why I choose these words. In such times, you mortals seek certainty and reason... justification, if you will. I am trying to give it."

Anita's smile vanished. "What times are you talking about, Uncle? And what do you mean, 'you mortals'?"

The man smiled subtly, slitting his eyes slightly as Gaitri sidled up alongside her sister. "You see me as your father's friend. But I have chosen his appearance to speak with you. I am not him. I am Yama, the god of death."

Gaitri gasped, but Anita laughed aloud. "Oh, Uncle! You're drunk again!"

But the man's face became expressionless, then darkened. The lines of his face deepened like geologic crevasses, his eyes sinking back into his head like dusty lunar craters. His nose seemed to retreat into his skull, sucking perception, air and hope with it. From the ether came a dry whisper, tinged with horror and ringing with a distraught desperation. It cried, *"Yaaaaahhhhhm."*

The world seemed to darken then, as the ghastly sigh echoed through the minds of both Anita and Gaitri. For that brief moment, there was no hope in the world, only despair. And this time it was Anita who gasped. "But if you are Yama, then..."

"Yes," said the god of death. "I have come..."

"For me?!" Anita cried.

"No," Yama replied. "For one who is not present but who is near. I have come for Nikhil, your betrothed."

Anita wailed and plunged her face into her hands, almost smashing her spectacles against the table top. Gaitri snatched her arm and tried her best to comfort her sister. Presently, Anita lifted her head, eyes moist and make-up runny. "This is a joke," she coughed, forcing an awkward smile. "Uncle, this is a joke and you are a cruel man."

"Call him," Yama said. He flicked a dismissive hand toward the two girls, his fingers long and bony.

Anita wrestled with her purse like a woman possessed, surfacing with her mobile phone, barely hanging on to it with her trembling hands. Somehow she managed to dial Nikhil's number. It rang. And rang. And rang six more times before Anita hung up. "Maybe he's asleep," she said aloud, clearly not believing what she was saying. "Or maybe he forgot to recharge the phone."

"Or maybe he doesn't want to answer it," Gaitri offered, and was ignored for her efforts.

Yama squinted in a surprisingly patient and grandfatherly way. "All of that may be true, yes. But you know in your heart that it isn't. Nikhil's life force, his soul, has been taken from his body. It happened as he napped at his desk. He felt no pain. I am here to collect that soul and take it to the other realm."

"You mean where it will be reborn? Reincarnationed? I mean, reincarnated?" Gaitri asked. Once more, she was ignored.

The lord of death forced a smile then began to rise from the picnic table. Anita lunged forward and snatched his hands. "Wait!" She cried. "You mean his soul is still here? That means he really isn't dead! You can give him back his soul, right?"

It was such a strange day for such talk. The sun was a brilliant yellow disc above the scene, beaming warmth

and joy down to the greenery below, where children frolicked, flowers exploded in colour, brooks babbled, lovers
spooned and birds sang. So much life and love surrounded
them. Yet so dour and dark were the content and context
of their words.

"Young lady," Yama spoke, as he extricated himself from
Anita's grip, finger by finger. "Against my better judgment
I have come here to offer some comfort. I did not go to
Nikhil's mother or to his father, nor his brothers or sisters.
I came to you, because I admire the way in which you
comport yourself." He frowned. "You should be proud
of it. You should be proud of how you have lived by the
old Hindu rules, even of how you and Nikhil have chosen
the full six-day wedding ceremony, though only one of the
days has been completed."

Anita sobbed pathetically, clearly lost for words and
comforts. Lord Yama glared judiciously into Anita's
pleading face, his own softening somewhat. "Because you
show such sorrow for your betrothed, I will allow you to
glimpse his essence, his soul." He reached into the thick
bush of grey hair that sprouted from his wizened scalp, and
delicately withdrew a glimmering thread.

"This," he said, "is Nikhil. It is all that matters about
him, his knowledge, experience, his love, memories and
values. It is essentially what you would call his soul. I per-

mit you to look upon it so that you might see the purity of the thing you mourn, so that you will know that he departed the realm of the living with faculties intact, that he enters the other realm whole. Take comfort in that."

But the otherworldly display did not have the effect Yama had desired. Instead of calming Anita, the sight of Nikhil's wormy soul, exposed and flapping in the air like a stray noodle from someone's discarded lunch, cast her into a new fit of wailing. She flung herself to the ground and grasped Yama's ankle as he turned and tried to walk away.

Gaitri, meanwhile, couldn't take her eyes off of Nikhil's "soul", as Yama carefully wove it back into his hair. Despite herself, she caught herself muttering, "Cool!"

"Lord Yama!" Anita exclaimed through snotty tears, still clutching the Dark Lord's ankle. "You said you approved of me and the way I have lived. Surely that warrants a favour?"

This time Yama bellowed in laughter. "Ah, the favour! Always, they ask for a favour, a boon!" Then he became serious again. "But the truth of it, girl, is that I do approve of you. And unlike the others who have asked, I might be convinced to grant you a favour. You see, I have watched you. I have seen that you have saved yourself for the sixth night of your wedding ceremony, while all about you others have abandoned that path, making light of the virginal marriage bed. In older times, your behaviour would have been expected. But in these 'modern' times, I'm afraid that you are exceptional. And because you are exceptional, I will grant you one favour. But you cannot wish for Nikhil or anyone else to come back to life. You may only ask for yourself."

Gaitri's eyes lit up. "'Nita!" she whispered loudly. "Money, 'Nita! Ask for money! Gazillions of it!"

But once more, Gaitri was ignored. "Okay," Anita said weakly, loosening her grip on the death god's ankle and rising to her feet, taking a moment to wipe her face, blow her nose and straighten her glasses. "I want perfect health for all my family members."

Yama sighed and smiled. "As always, Anita, you choose others before yourself. But the favour I give must only be for you, not for others. So, instead I will give you –and you alone—perfect health."

To Gaitri's ears, though, Anita's answer had been canny. Nikhil was essentially family, and his perfect health would necessarily mean him not being dead! The god of death was not so clever or perceptive, after all.

A remarkable thing happened then. Anita seemed to grow several years younger instantaneously. Her skin glowed with moist vitality; the whites of her eyes appeared bleached and unblemished; her soft belly firmed somewhat; and she stood taller and straighter than ever before! Then she began to squint weirdly, finally snatching her spectacles –now more a hindrance than an aid—and throwing them to the ground.

Gaitri watched in astonishment. It was real! This really was Yama, a god of heaven! "Darn it, 'Nita," she said to her sister, "You should have asked for the money!"

The god of death turned away from the sisters and, with one bony hand, reached out and pinched the air. Where his fingers met, a tiny black pucker appeared, floating above the ground. It swirled like a silent vortex, growing with each turn, till at last it was the size of a door. Beyond the door, there was nothing but sparkling lights and a hint of sound. Gaitri thought she heard an autumn breeze or the gurgle of a fast-running creek. She knew –they all knew—that this was the doorway to the other realm.

As Yama took his first step toward the doorway, Anita rushed to block him. "No, my lord," she pleaded. "Please, there must be a way. You said you approved of the way I have lived my life. Surely, you can't ruin my life now by taking away my beloved?"

Yama sighed again. "Your generation greatly disappoints me," he said. "But, as I said, you have behaved well. Also, you have kept your hair long and you conceal your body from lecherous eyes, unlike others of your years. This, perhaps, also warrants a favour. But the same conditions apply. You may only ask for yourself."

"Yes!" Gaitri exclaimed, pumping her fist in the air. "The money, 'Nita. Ask for the money!"

But Anita, ever stoic, pushed out her chin, and said, "My lord, I ask that I shall never know sorrow."

Gaitri cringed. "A bit obvious, don't you think, 'Nita?"

But Yama did not waiver. "Of course, child. Let it be so. You shall never know or feel sorrow."

Anita beamed, convinced that her shallow ploy had been successful. "Then how can you take my beloved from me? Will that not cause me sorrow?"

Yama looked to the ground, as would a disappointed mentor whose favourite student had just posed a naïve question. "It is true that you will not feel sorrow when I take Nikhil's soul through to the other realm. But you will feel despair, regret, wistfulness, depression and a host of other unpleasant emotions, all of which are quite natural and expected."

He smiled then, inhaled sharply, and announced, "Okay, enough wastage of time. I have other appointments, you know. The retirement home in the West End is long overdue a culling. Chin up, child. Widowhood can have its rewards, as well. Dedicate your life to charity or travel or something." And he took another step toward the doorway.

"Wait!" Gaitri screamed at the top of her lungs. This time, both adults took notice of her. They waited for her to speak, but she needed a moment to gather her thoughts. "Look, um, Mr Yama. 'Nita-*didi* is the best big sister in the world. She looks after me and everyone else and never asks for anything in return. The only thing that she has ever wanted for herself is Nikhil. He's the only present that she needs or wants. So, um, I think you should give him back. Because, um, it's the right thing to do."

Yama watched her crookedly. To Gaitri it looked as if he were watching a talking dog or a monkey in a zoo. With some difficulty, she repressed the urge to stick out her tongue.

Yama then turned to Anita and examined her features for a while. "Well," he finally said, "The respect of one's younger siblings is also sadly rare in this world. And because of it, I will grant you, Anita, one final favour. This is it. There will be no more. My patience is not long at the best of times, and now it is truly at an end. So, you will receive this final boon, with the same conditions attached, as before."

"Let me think..." Anita said.

"No," Yama interrupted. "You will not choose. The little one will choose for you." He indicated Gaitri with the dismissive wave of one of his bony hands.

"Me?" Gaitri inquired, wide-eyed and incredulous.

"Yes you," Yama said. "Now, please. Choose now." Anita looked imploringly at her little sister, both of them positively terrified.

"All right," Gaitri said. "I wish that 'Nita-*didi* will have many many children so that I can be an Auntie. I wish that the she will have 14 babies!"

No one spoke as the universe stood still. A god posed in contemplative silence. Above him, the clouds ceased to move and the birds no longer chirped. Behind him, the doorway to the death swirled in silence. And about him, two mortals watched in immobile horror, afraid to breathe lest the last glimmers of hope fade from their world. At last, the muscles at the sides of his mouth quivered, and words rushed from between his lips. "That is a fair request, child," he said. "Let it be done."

"And?" Gaitri nudged.

"And what?"

"Well," Gaitri said, "How can 'Nita-*didi* have children if you take her husband away?"

At that, Lord Yama grinned broadly, displaying wide, yellowy teeth. Then, to everyone's surprise, he bellowed in laughter. But death and laughter are unfamiliar companions, and to mortal ears the bellow sounded more like the thunder of ocean waves crashing into a seaside cliff: loud and impressive, but fraught with danger and violence.

Yama spoke. "You have indeed bested me child. I am a creature of my word. So that my promise to Anita might be fulfilled, I return Nikhil's soul to his body, that he might be father to fourteen children." One more, he plucked Nikhil's soul from his scalp and held it delicately between his right thumb and forefinger. Placing the glowing noodle against his lips, he gave a wet, godly exhalation that sent it dancing into the winds, blown back to Nikhil's supine body, which still lay slumped at his desk.

Moments later, Anita's mobile phone was ringing. It was Nikhil, wondering how he had missed her earlier call. "Must have fallen asleep," he concluded, in his drowsy, clueless way.

Without another word, Lord Yama turned and marched through the vortex doorway, sealing it instantly behind him. He was gone, as if he had never been. Yet his presence lingered, as it always does.

"Gaitri!" Anita sang, as she rushed forward to embrace her heroic sister. "I was afraid you were going to ask for the money!"

"That Yama fellow was not very smart," Gaitri muttered between sisterly squeezes.

"What do you mean?"

"I mean, you could have had the babies with someone else, right? It didn't have to be Nikhil. Or you could have adopted. Like I said, not very smart."

"That's right, Gaitri," Anita said, stroking her sister's hair and kissing her everywhere she could reach. "Death is stupid, pointless, unfair, old fashioned and patronizing. But he's not unconquerable after all, na?" Then she pinched Gaitri softly on her bottom.

"Ouch! What was that for?" Gaitri complained.

"That was for asking for fourteen babies. Two would have been sufficient, you know!" Hand-in-hand and warmed by laughter and love, they walked to the sandbox to help Jai find his lost marbles. □

Chapter Seven

Lords of Izzat

I see them when the house lights first go down and the theatre is lighted only by the glare from the screen, a collage of technicolour hues that spits opening credits with a rhythm kept by the standard action musical theme.

I see them pressed together, wrapped in the blanket of false privacy gifted by the darkened theatre. They touch tentatively, then with more confidence, her ear upon his shoulder, his cheek upon her head.

I see them yet I cannot believe my eyes. Why does no one react? They crouch in intimacy, huddle in sexual conspiracy, remain seemingly oblivious to the crowd around them, a crowd able and willing to rip them to pieces.

I see them and my back stiffens. My two friends, my lads, have not yet noticed, it seems, so caught up are they in the images on the screen: dancing girls, heroic boys, suffering old folk, nefarious all-powerful villains and, of course, the happy choreography of so many hummable songs. All this has drawn my lads' attention away from the abomination squeezed into the corner, two rows before us.

Amitabh fills the screen, his powerful voice matched only by the virile landscape of his face and form, resplendent in straight lines, deliberate creases and, everywhere, length and lankiness. He fills me with confidence and testosterone. He tells me why I am a man.

I see them look up at Amitabh, smile, then return to their cuddling. The play of cinematic light upon their features confirms my suspicions. She is as the rest of us, a young Indian seeking love and protection. But he is the other. His shade is subtle enough to pass as one of us, his features sufficiently ambiguous. But there is something that gives him away --the dancing eyes above the high cheekbones, the skin a tad too dark and the hair a tad too curly. He is black, we are Indian and this is Guyana in a time when such is not allowed.

Amitabh clenches his fist as he witnesses a dishonour done to his woman. The camera zooms in to his slitting eyes, and his tempered fury simmers from beneath them. Therein lies explosive danger, but it will be unleashed in measured bouts, calculated for optimal effect, destruction and sweet retribution.

I feel my own blood boil, my lips pressing together so hard the colour no doubt drains from them. But, of course, no one can see, for we are engulfed in dark.

There's a thing that happens in the cinema, a small and elegant thing. The darkness descends, the rectangle at the front of the room glows with hallucinogenic warmth, and a dream fills your head. In the cloying heat of the Georgetown summer, this is a cool, transporting reprieve, wherein voyages are undertaken, fantasies given flesh and life lessons transmitted via archetypes and morality plays.

When Madhuri offers her life in exchange for that of her son, she is an example for all women, who must be idealized and martyred before the divine pedestals of their children. When Amitabh vows revenge, he is the masculine paragon, filled with retributive power: divine justice incarnate.

And when they gather beneath the silvery moonlight, bedecked in Asian finery and with heartfelt expressions carved melodramatically into their impossibly beautiful faces, the song is sure to erupt. In all its incarnations, it brings together the disparate, rhythmically taps the collective chest, and —magically, incomprehensibly, certainly improbably——reaches up to the gods, for they of heaven are spoken to only by prayer and music; and by action.

My gods demand action. This Indian girl must be redeemed and her intransigence righted. Such is the way of
this world, this place and this time.

I see them settle ever more comfortably into the curves
of one another's bodies. On the screen, a young man sings
a ballad to his beloved, but she rebukes him coyly, playing
the sexual game as expertly as it has been played by cour-
tesans for centuries: beckon then admonish, suggest then
deny. The young man plays willingly, in full knowledge of
his erstwhile lover's manipulative ways. It is the dance of
sex, so oft mistaken for the dance of love.

The black boy hums along to the Hindi tune, though
he cannot possibly know the words. Nor can any of us,
separated as we are from India by oceans and generations.
But we sing along nonetheless, all of us.

His brown girl bobs her head in time, the two of them
locked into the rhythm, reprising the on-screen courtship
dance in their eyes and spirits. They engage in coitus in
their hearts if not their bodies, drawn to a sexual union by
the dancing courtesan's viral song.

It is one of our songs, one of our dances. I know this
because the dancers are brown. The women wear sarees.
The men wear moustaches and gesture broadly in that
special Indian way. And they sing in Hindi, the language
of my ancestors. It is for us alone, for me. Not for him.

But he sings along, as does the whole theatre. My fists clench and I glance at my lads, ready to alert them, to launch the attack. There are broad grins plastered to their shining faces, their chins nodding so slightly in time with the courtesan's dance. They too are caught in her web, drawn in by her ancient cotillion.

So, I wait, letting the fantasy linger a while longer.

Amitabh thrashes the goons who stand in his way. Flashing images of his dead son, his dishonoured wife, show us the thoughts in his head. He is driven by both grief and rage, but more accurately by honour –izzat— that unique indescribable thing that young men hover about, yet never truly manage to hold in the immobile, loitering grip of their conscious, focused contemplation. We all strive for it, are driven by it, rationalize actions by citing it, but none of us can define it.

Honour, sex and love. Really, there is no more.

We are approaching the climax. The audience feels it. There is renewed stillness and silence, broken by the singular shuffle of fabric as couples slide closer together. A particularly energetic dance number has heated our blood, its subtext less sexual and playful and more worrisome and foreboding. We have been primed for resolution.

Our hero finds his transgressor, bursts into his office and beats his goons into submission. The villain is held by his collars, at virtue's mercy. Our man slaps him about and we are shown the cocked and loaded gun in his right hand.

But Amitabh sets the villain free in a moment of suspended silence, broken only by the wetness of breaths. Our hero marches out of the office, stumbles really. He lets his gun fall to the ground, unused. In the foreground, the villain, now partially redeemed, sobs in grief and regret: with the realization of lost honour comes the first steps toward its reclamation.

A final cathartic dance number, the traditional cinematic denouement, and the credits roll. But people are already standing, leaving.

I see them kiss, ever so briefly, hidden behind the shuffle of bustling silhouettes. My lads, their grins almost solar in intensity, remain oblivious. But I continue to stare, and they do not think to follow my gaze. My lads are my compass and meaning and reason, for together we strive for izzat, that thing so effortlessly lifted and shaped by the heroes that appear only in this room. Somehow, the heroes, these giants of light and colour, grasp it, stretch it, speak it and fold it into cloaks, guns, tears, love and action. They are the lords of izzat, its gurus, and we their undeserving pupils.

I see them stand, at last, and slowly make their way to the exit, barely touching now, their heads a bit low, as if they are aware that their transgression has been witnessed. Yet they both glow with relaxed contentment, an aura so incandescent that I can see it in the darkened theatre. They reach the swinging door and push through into the hot brightness, like fraternal twins emerging from the wet, dark birth canal. I see them slip through and disappear into the light.

And I do nothing. □

Chapter Eight

Rupinder

"It's as high as Mount Kailash!"

"No, it's not, Kultar. It's only as high as a couple of houses. We can climb it."

"You can barely climb into your hammock, Maneesh. Look: no handholds, no ledges, nothing for leverage. We can't climb that. Well, maybe I can, but certainly not the two of you." Kultar Singh stroked his magnificent beard and considered the foreboding structure. It was smooth brick, about 40 feet high, with no door. At the very top, though, was an open window barely wide enough for a man to climb through.

"Yes, Kultar can climb it," Jageesh said. "I once saw him climb the face of a cliff with no rope! He's like a spider, this Sikh. A regular makkad-wallah!"

Kultar glared at him. "Sorry," Maneesh said, backing away. "I meant Makkad-wallah *Singh*!"

Maneesh nodded. "Yes, Kultar. You can do it. Remember, man: the gold is in a box by the wall. That's what the fellow said, na. That's all we know."

Kultar rolled his eyes. Maneesh and his "fellows" always knew where gold was supposed to be hidden. The gold had a habit of growing legs and walking away just before they arrived, though.

"Well," Maneesh said. "We'd better get to it. The master of this place gets back at sundown, which is not too far off. If we're caught, it's the gallows for sure."

Kultar stripped off his kurta and slung the trio's only loop of rope over his shoulder. Taking a deep breath, he climbed onto the backs of his two friends, then launched his massive form onto the tower, magically sticking to the sheer brick like the spider-man to which his friends had likened him. Beneath him, Maneesh and Jageesh had been thrown into the thick mud, and they struggled to find footing again. Maneesh's pet rabbit remained clean and dry inside his pocket, though.

Inch by inch, Kultar crawled up the tower, spread-eagled and lubricated with torrents of his sweat. Thirty agonizing minutes later, he was at the ledge of the window. With a last rush of strength, he hoisted his almost 7 foot frame into the tiny room, and beheld its uninspiring contents. It was an unlit bedroom, with a dusty straw-stuffed mattress and a couple of books littering the unswept floor. And there was no door, no exit. But against the far wall, just as Maneesh had insisted, there was a wide brass box.

Clearly, this was a place for the master to sit and guard his treasure. How the master got in and out was anyone's guess. Maybe he travelled with his own 30 foot ladder. Or maybe he sprouted wings and flew.

Kultar rushed over to the box and tried to open it, but it was sealed shut. "Throw it out the window!" Maneesh commanded. Kultar tried to lift it, but despite his inhuman strength, he could barely get a corner off the ground.

"I'm going to need help!" he called down to his companions. Maneesh nodded and beckoned for Kultar to drop an end of the rope down to him. He did so, but even has he hung himself halfway out the window, the rope dangled about 12 feet from the ground.

But Maneesh would not be denied. His shrewd little eyes squinted as his brain hatched a plan. "Look," he said, after some minutes of thought. "My brother Jageesh here is a fine tumbler. I will bend over and he will leap onto my back and up to the rope." Kultar shrugged.

As planned, Jageesh took a running start and bounded onto his brother's back. In one continuous motion, he launched himself upward, barely managing to snatch the rope that Kultar dangled from the window. With several mighty heaves, the enormous Sikh pulled the little gymnast the rest of the way into the tiny room, both men collapsing into a sweaty, huffing mess.

Then they took another crack at the box. Even with both men heaving, they were barely able to drag it to the window. It would be impossible for only two of them to toss it out. "We're going to need more help!" they called down to Maneesh.

"All right," Maneesh said. "Let's think this through." Once more, he adopted his contemplation posture, eyes slitted, forehead creased and mouth pursed. This time he added the tapping of a foot, which was difficult in the thick mud.

"Hurry up!" Jageesh called to his brother. "The sun is going down soon. The master will return!"

Maneesh bellowed back: "Look here, Jageesh. You hold the rope down, and Kultar will dangle you by your feet. That way the rope will reach the ground."

"What?!" Jageesh exclaimed, backing away from the window in horror. But Kultar picked him up with one arm and flung him, wailing and thrashing, over the window, holding Jageesh's knees to his own chest while weaving the rope down with his free hand.

Through terrified barks of protest, Jageesh nonetheless managed to grasp the rope and dangle it to the ground. But even with Maneesh jumping for it, the rope was still a few inches beyond his hands.

After several failed attempts, and much whining on Jageesh's part, the two atop the tower slumped to the ground to rest and consider their options. They could think of none. "I have one more idea!" Maneesh suddenly called up.

"What now?" Kultar asked, quite fed up with his friend's plans.

"Well..." Maneesh seemed to hesitate. "Back in the Christian school, they told me of a white lady who lived in a tower like this. She was locked up good, yes? But when her boyfriend came to visit, she would drop her long hair to the ground and he would climb up! Then she would entertain him with her womanly tenderness until it was time for him to leave, which he would do by climbing down her hair again."

"Ohhhhhhh!" Jageesh sighed. "Such a woman!"

"So what?" Kultar demanded. "This strumpet is not here, na? What good is she to us?"

"What was her name?" Jageesh asked dreamily, ignoring Kultar. "Did she marry the fellow? Is she single still?"

Maneesh continued: "Her name was Zapunder... or R upindaal..."

"Rupinder?" Jageesh offered, hoping for a good Punjabi woman.

"Yes!" Maneesh agreed. "That must be it. Rupinder. So, we don't have the lovely Rupinder here. But we have the lovely Kultar, with hair so long we can sleep in it like a hammock!"

Jageesh turned to the big Sikh, a grin stretching ear to ear. "Kultar Rupinder! Come give me a kiss!" Jageesh laughed so hard that he coughed and sputtered. Kultar glared menacingly at him. "Oh sorry!" Jageesh said, backing away from the big man. "I meant Kultar Rupinder *Singh*!"

Kultar sprang to his feet and shook his fist at Maneesh on the ground. "If you or your monkey brother mock the gurus again I will cut open your bellies and I will have your rabbit for my supper!"

"We mock no one, mighty Singh," Maneesh said. "But your hair is long and tough. We can use it as a rope."

"You stupid dwarf. My hair is barely 5 feet long."

"Look," Maneesh explained. "Tie the rope to the end of your hair, then Jageesh will help you hang your freakishly large body from the ledge. Then the rope will reach the ground." Don't think, you'll hurt yourself. Let me do the thinking.

Kultar clenched his fists and opened his mouth to respond, but Jageesh cut him off. "We don't have time to argue. It's almost sundown. Come on, let's do this, my sweet Rupinder." The big Sikh scowled sheer hatred, but kept his mouth shut, and dutifully began the process of unwinding his immaculately oiled and coiled locks from beneath his turban.

After some effort, they managed to tie the rope to the end of his hair, and tossed it out the window. Kultar's neck jerked with the force of the rope pulling taut. Next, the Sikh hung his torso out the window, with Jageesh clutching his legs for counterbalance.

With some effort, the tips of Maneesh's fingers could just brush the end of the rope. Thursting up from his toes, he gingerly grasped the rope and hung his whole weight from it, his pet rabbit scurrying nervously inside his coat.

An otherworldly scream erupted from Kultar's mouth as he felt his scalp begin to tear. He quickly grabbed the base of his locks to ease the pressure. "God!" he cried. "What insanity is this? Let go, you lunatic!"

"Kultar, don't be a baby," Maneesh chided, as he scurried up the rope as quickly as he could. "Is a white lady tougher than you, O mighty warrior? Did the real Rupinder have a better fighting spirit?"

Kultar roared his mightiest battle roar, and with several superhuman heaves managed to pull Maneesh all the way into the tiny room.

While Jageesh and the Sikh caught their breaths, Maneesh immediately took to examining the brass box. Like the others, he could find no way to force it open. "Yes," he concluded. "We shall have to toss it out the window. The impact will force it open."

The three of them took hold of box and strained to lift it to the ledge. It was an awkward task, made more so by the sweat of their bodies, which made the box slippery, and by the waning light of the setting sun. Finally, they had it teetering on the window's ledge. And with one shared glance between them, they let it plummet to the ground. It struck the mud with an unimpressive hollow slap, splashing wet dirt in all directions; but it remained sealed.

Kultar stared down at the unopened box in disbelief. Then he turned to Maneesh, ferocity bleeding through his pores, and murderous rage beaming from his reddened eyes.

"It should have opened!" Maneesh pleaded, leaning out the window to escaped Kultar's grasp.

"What do we do now?" Jageesh asked, interjecting himself between the two. "The box is down there. We're up here. The master is on his way. What do we do?"

"That's easy," Maneesh offered, thankful for a topic to distract Kultar from his fury. "We get the rope and lower ourselves down...."

Now, Maneesh was not very athletic. Indeed, his brother had inherited more than his fair share of strength and suppleness, leaving Maneesh with an imbalanced, dwarfish body, offset only by a devious and crafty mind. So it was not surprising that the act of simply sitting on the window ledge, albeit leaning away from Kultar and toward the open, would be sufficient to send him over the edge. Indeed, Maneesh's face seemed frozen in stupefying fear. He floated, seemingly in slow motion, backwards and downwards toward the muddy ground. Miraculously, his foot had become entangled in one end of the rope, and Jageesh leapt, just in time to snatch the other end. But not being a particularly strong man, he too was pulled out of the window by his brother's plummeting weight.

Kultar, the only one strong enough to save them both, acted as quickly as he could. He extruded his whole torso from the window, locking his feet against the wall, and amazingly managed to get hold of Jageesh's pants leg. But it was cheap cotton that easily ripped. Both brothers fell to the mud, fortunately avoiding the sharp edges of the brass box, and leaving Kultar alone in the tower room, bewildered and holding a piece of torn pants leg.

"Brothers!" Kultar called from on high, his long hair whipped by the wind and looking quite ethereal in the diminishing light of dusk. "Are you alive?"

"Yes," Jageesh replied weakly. "Unless you are an apparition of the white angel Rupinder and not Kultar the makkad-wallah."

Kultar growled back, "Is your precious Rupinder-ji 7 feet tall with a beard, you fool?"

"Sorry... Makkad-wallah *Singh*."

Maneesh rubbed his ankles then shakily got to his feet, looking like so much the highwayman scoundrel now that he was bent over and covered in mud. "Come on, Jageesh, let's get the horses and pull this thing home."

"What about me?!" Kultar called from the window. "How will I get down? If I jump, my weight will kill me!"

"What about you?" Maneesh sneered. "We don't need you anymore." He gestured for Jageesh to get to his feet and follow him.

Then, from the darkness came the sound of hoofbeats. From the bushes emerged four men on horseback. Each was resplendent in silken kurtas and armed with swords. One even carried a gun; it was tucked into the front of his silver-lined belt, and matched well the metallic sheen of his jewelled turban. He was, without a doubt, the master of the tower.

The master dismounted and marched pointedly to his box. Maneesh and Jageesh stood still in terror, while Kultar ducked into the shadows within the room.

The master bent to the box and located a tiny keyhole near one edge. With a golden key that he lifted from a string about his neck, he opened the lock and threw back the lid. "I see you've succeeded in stealing my ladder," he said.

Maneesh looked into the box, eyes skinned wide like full moons. In the box was a heavy ship's anchor, and twined around it a tough old rope ladder. There was nothing more.

"My treasure is still safe in the tower," the master said. "But you have still stolen from me. We go now to justice." His men hopped off their horses and took Maneesh and Jageesh forcefully, binding their hands and tying them to the saddles.

The master and his men re-mounted and led the brothers off into the night. As they lurched and jerked, Maneesh realized his pet rabbit was no longer in his sleeve. Casting a final glance back to the tower's window, he saw Kultar singh hold the little rodent up to the emerging moon, smacking his lips in culinary anticipation.

Maneesh growled in fury. "Rupinder!" he cried. "Rupinder, let down my hare!"

But Kultar Singh ignored him. As his foot brushed the straw-filled mattress, he felt that it was harder than it should be. A little more prodding revealed that the mattress was stuffed with something other than straw, something metallic and heavy. Gold, perhaps?

Now, all he had to do was find a way down. Makkad-wallah would find a way, he was certain. □

Chapter Nine

The Nadan's New Clothes

"You know what day is today?" Amma teased. Karuna smiled dutifully and even tried to blush. "You know, yes?"

"Yes, Amma," Karuna said. "It is Pongal!" Despite himself, his smile spread across his face, betraying the genuine joy that the festival inspired within him.

Had they still been in the village, the girls would be busily adorning the cows with dyes and blossoms, while Karuna and his Appa would be trying to construct a fake bed of arrows, upon which Appa would then lie, mimicking the death scene of Lord Bhishma, who was said to have chosen Pongal as his moment of death after having been pierced with one of Lord Arjuna's unerring arrows.

Karuna would always be reminded of the storybook Appa kept amongst his clothes, the one illustrated with wet hues of dull blue and deep red. In it was an evocative drawing of legendary and ancient Bhishma, the most respected and feared prince of the mythical realm, spiritual father to his great clan, sprawled atop the array of sharp arrays, his naked loins strategically concealed by a passing warrior.

"Prince Arjuna, you have slain me with your arrow!" Appa would exclaim in mock despair, arranging himself atop his flimsy construction. Karuna would then attempt to pull his father from the arrow bed, only to himself be pinned and tickled, usually resulting in a muddy wrestling match into which his cousins and brothers would jump. It was one ritual piled atop another.

One time, Appa's loosely tied lungi had fallen off during the wrestling bout. Amma had looked positively scandalized, and all the onlooking village girls had shielded their eyes in horror. (Though Karuna was certain some had peeked!) But Appa, ever the clown, frolicked in his nakedness, continued to chase the boys and proclaimed, "If Lord Bhishma could fight naked, then so can I!" The storybook drawing bright in their memories, they had grappled and laughed till Appa's younger brother Kavalan had managed to pry him away with promises of rum.

Squatting on the kitchen floor, Karuna fingered the feeble arrows he had glued together from matches and toothpicks. They were not of the quality Appa would have made. But in the village Appa had had access to trees and branches. Here in the city, Karuna only had what the local tobacco shop could provide.

Uncle Kavalan looked down on the arrows with a heavy brow. "I don't think you could shoot a cockroach with those," he said. Amma doused him with a disapproving look.

Karuna frowned. "It's not for cockroaches. A roach cannot play Bhishma."

"Then who? Who will be Bhishma?" Kavalan was teasing, of course. There was only one choice. Karuna leapt to his feet with a matchbook arrow in hand, and smashed its crumpled end into Kavalan's chest, the boy's bony body sinking into the older man's big embracing arms.

"Haha! You have slain me with your arrow, Prince Arjuna!" Kavalan laughed aloud and squeezed Karuna to his chest, sustaining the forced moment of joy, and mimicking Appa as Appa would have mimicked Bhishma.

Amma slapped the two of them on their backs good naturedly. "That's enough, you men. They will be marching the cows soon."

Karuna was taken aback. "They will still march the cows in here? In the city?"

"I don't know how others do it. But we are still stupid village people and we will do our stupid village things." Karuna was not sure if Amma was being sarcastic, but he didn't care. The procession of adorned cows was a connection to his old life, and he would revel in it. But first, he must complete the bed of arrows.

"Leave that!" Amma commanded. "Go put on your new clothes for the procession!"

"New clothes?"

"Yes! The Nadan is coming, too! We must dress properly, not like poor village folk."

Karuna frowned at this, but dutifully reported to his bed. Upon it lay a brand-new lungi and angavastram, each bright white in exquisite newness and cleanliness. Uncle Kavalan perched himself on the edge of the bed and smiled knowingly. "Stiff cotton, yes?"

Karuna nodded.

"Not good for wrestling in the mud, na?" He grinned warmly.

"Hurry!" Amma shouted from the kitchen. "The procession is almost here and you don't want to miss it." Karuna shrugged on the new clothes, though clearly did not enjoy doing so. "Look at the Nadan," Amma continued, peering through the window onto the street. "He is so radiant in his golden dhoti and slippers!"

Uncle Kavalan sniffed. "The man is rich from our rent, yes? And yet we must still shrink from the glare of his ridiculous clothes."

It was true, Karuna knew: the Nadan held the lease to all the homes in the burrough. All the children were rehearsed to be on their best behaviour when the Nadan approached. He was, as he was fond of announcing, "father to the community."

The Nadan was known for his fragile ego. One time, Kavalan's bicycle had splashed mud on the Nadan's shoes, and Kavalan had seen his rent increased that very same day. The same fate had befallen their neighbour, who had once failed to compliment the Nadan's new hat. And there were rumours of worse reprisals that had been handed to neighbours who had done nothing more than fail to greet the great man upon passing him in the street. If indeed the Nadan was leading this procession, Karuna understood that it was a good idea to at least be seen to be watching.

"Go, go!" Amma came from behind and brushed Karuna out of the house and onto the street, just as he reached for a handful of his shoddy "arrows".

Karuna found himself in the midst of the procession of cows, each cleverly decorated with turmeric bindis and garlanded ears. The ground was already ripe with fresh dung, and the streets laced with gawking admirers, each enjoying Pongal in their own way.

He ran into the throng of cows, allowing himself to dodge their heads and haunches, occasionally slipping his toes into the warm dung. Amma cringed at this, fearing for Karuna's fresh new clothes. But she understood: this was a taste of the village life that had been torn from the boy, just as his Appa had been.

He dashed and dodged, and gradually something resembling joy took hold of him. After a bit, he approached the head of the procession, just as it was looping back toward his house. There, for the first time, he caught a glimpse of the Nadan.

The fat, middle-aged man marched like a band leader, a functionless baton tucked under his arm. Most noticeably, he was bedecked in an astonishingly gaudy golden dhoti that glimmered in the sun and puffed out to hide his expanding hindquarters. Over his shoulder was slung an equally golden angavastram. And beneath his feet were the slightest of slippers, formed of actual gold leaf.

As he marched, his nose was pushed to the sky, and his greasy moustache seemed to squirm across his lip like a listless caterpillar. Against his better judgement, Karuna could not help but stare in deep fascination.

Then the procession rounded back past Karuna's house, where both Kavalan and Amma stood watching, hands prepared to applaud both the cows and the Nadan's inflated finery. What happened next seemed to unfold in slow motion.

As Karuna watched, the Nadan took deeper and more deliberate steps, his nose still pointed to the sun. He could not see the enormous bolus of fresh dung that awaited his descending slipper. As his foot struck the stuff, blobs of hot cow refuse splashed upward, soiling the fringes of the Nadan's new dhoti. Noticing this, he let his baton slip down his thigh, then reflexively reached to catch it. But he missed, throwing his bean-shaped body even more out of kilter. His right foot twisted and slipped back, finding purchase in yet another impressive pile of redolent dung. This time, the splash covered the entire rear of his dhoti and caused the Nadan to flail wildly, struggling to keep balance.

As the fracas unfolded, the Nadan's mouth opened in a silent scream, and his hands searched fruitlessly for some sort of support. What they found instead was his exquisite angavastram, which he yanked downward. It fell to the ground and was promptly trampled by cows. The Nadan made an ill-advised move to retrieve the piece of cloth, but only managed to loosen his dhoti through his awkward bending.

And as Karuna and all the other assembled celebrants looked on in horror, the Nadan's golden dhoti sank to his ankles. There he stood, as naked as the day he was born, stinking of dung and bathed in the sunbeams of the noon day, which shone comically upon his nether parts like an unflinching theatrical spotlight.

The silence probably lasted only a second or two, but it seemed to all present like twenty minutes or more. The Nadan's gaze had fallen first upon Uncle Kavalan, then upon Karuna's Amma. Familiar creases of rage had begun to form in the centre of the Nadan's forehead, and his teeth were now bared beneath his wormy moustache.

Karuna looked to his uncle and mother and saw the profound sense of despair that had befallen them. The dung that the Nadan had slipped upon had been located directly in front of their house. They were responsible.

Flinging his own cotton angavastram aside, he raced to the very front of the procession and launched himself against the Nadan, dramatically crumpling his matchbook "arrow" into the Nadan's bared chest.

The older man stared at him in confusion.

Uncle Kavalan ran forward and clapped his hands together slowly. "P-prince Arjuna," he said nervously, "Congratulations. You have slain Lord Bhishma with your ar-row!"

Quickly, the onlookers caught on and joined in the ap-plause and congratulations. An unsteady smile began to spread across the Nadan's weathery face, as he came to understand that as "father of the community", what better role to play than Bhishma, grand-sire of kings?

And as the revelers danced away with the Nadan, who still pranced in his nakedness, Uncle Kavalan grasped Karuna about the waist and dragged him into the mud, wrestling and grappling as if Appa himself were holding them down with his strong hands and warm words. □

Chapter Ten

Drawing Dead People

S itting atop the sand of a featureless beach just before dawn, his silhouette was the most prominent figure to be seen. Crouched facing the water, his head seemed to radiate a purply-pink halo as if it were set against the distant glow of the submerged sun.

She started to walk to him.

A stroll of ten or fifteen metres seemed the length of a marathon. She spent the time contemplating the possible results of disturbing his solitude. The sound of the sand squishing between her toes was deafening. It was so un-rhythmic and out of place when heard against the gentle splashing of the tide.

"I thought I'd find you here."

He looked up slowly, not surprised at all. "Why were you looking for me?"

"Just want someone to talk to. Mind if I join you?" She didn't wait for an answer, just deposited herself next to him on the soft moist sand. She felt a slight chill along her skin, and smelled the early morning crispness in the air. The warmth of his body was comforting on one side of her; the other side bristled against the ocean breeze.

The water was flat. There were no islands or ships to see, no waves swelling above the horizon. The peace was almost disquieting. It wasn't natural, she reflected, for human beings to be so peaceful, so at rest. "What are you doing here?" she asked him.

"Watching the water."

"No, I mean *here*, in French Guiana."

"Same thing as you." He shrugged. "I'm trying to save giant sea turtles. That's what the brochure said, right?"

She rolled her eyes. "Okay, be that way."

A few of the bolder stars were still visible, daring to risk drowning by the imminent flood of sunlight. No one else was awake yet. But soon the new day would begin. With the morning light, the ecology team would drudge back to the work of tagging turtles, fuelled by life-giving caffeine and a sometimes-pathetic do-gooder attitude. And as the day unfolded, they would toil much too hard to appreciate the subtle beauty of the place.

She tried again. "Each of us is running from something," she said. "We ran away from the real world."

"This is the real world."

"Yes, I know, but..."

"No buts. This beach has been here for millions of years. And, after we're gone, it'll be here for millions more. When we die, our flesh will turn to sand, and our blood will turn to water. We all go back to the beach eventually."

"Don't get sappy on me. I hate that shit." She was quiet again, a bit ashamed. "Sure, this is the real natural world," she finally said, "But it's not the world we're used to. We're both from cities. The city is our real world, right?"

"Then why don't you go back?"

She didn't answer for a while. The question might have been rhetorical. Really, who would want to go back? Sure, here there was dysentery, poverty and hard beds. But back home there weren't any sunrises like this one. She tried a new tack. "What did you do...in the real world?" she asked.

"What did *you* do?"

She groaned inwardly. "I was an architect. Mostly for condominiums." He didn't comment. So, she continued. "I think I built some beautiful buildings, you know? Yeah, condos can be a blight. But I made a real effort to beautify the city, to make it a nice place to be..."

"Is this a nice place to be?"

"Yes! Of course. This is the best place I've ever been. It's clean, sweet, fresh... effortless. The place is beautiful, the turtles are.... Amazing. And the people..."

He turned to her, anticipating. But she looked straight ahead and measured her words. "The people here are friendly."

"Yes," he agreed. "The people are friendly. Do you really think that a pretty building is better than an ugly building?"

"What do you mean?"

"I mean they're both buildings. They're both collections of concrete and rubber and steel, regardless of how they're shaped."

She wanted to object, to complain again of his annoying correctness, but said nothing. This time maybe it was appropriate.

The sun was peeking its head slightly over the horizon now, visible rays of reddish light reaching forth to touch the other side of the world. Those last bold stars were quickly extinguished, and welcomed rays beamed upon their chilled flesh.

There was warmth in the air.

"So, what did *you* do in the real world?"

He waited before answering, surveying the glistening water peaks with a keen unflinching glare. "I don't know what to say. I did a lot of things. I wasn't a high society architect like you, or a lawyer or doctor like some of the other guys here. I did whatever I felt like doing."

"Like?"

"Once I took a job drawing dead people."

"I don't understand," she said.

"You know. When a death occurs, the police draw a chalk line around the corpse, right? Well, I was the guy who did the drawing."

She didn't react. She just looked at him, perhaps a bit skeptically. But he went on.

"I saw some really interesting ways that people die. One guy had his testicles crushed in a vice before being shot him in the head. That one was pretty easy because I didn't have to draw the vice, just the intact body parts."

Despite herself, she kept her composure.

"Once," he continued, "I had to draw a little girl who had suffocated inside an oven. Turns out it wasn't a homicide, just an unfortunate game of hide-and-seek."

The sun was more than halfway above the horizon now, and she could see from his sagging face that he had been up all night. It was easy to forget the passing of time here.

Everything was so slow, so removed from manmade clocks and alarms and schedules that here it was easy to ignore one's mortality. Daily interaction with nearly immortal sea turtles certainly aided that illusion. Thoughts of death and degeneration were escapable.

"Once," he said, "I took a job as a subway operator. Just for a couple of weeks. I quit after one guy jumped in front of the train I was driving, and another guy got stuck between the closing doors and was dragged across the platform."

"What happened to him?"

"His arm was ripped off when the train entered the tunnel." She touched his arm. It was warm. Surprisingly.

"Come on," she said. "Let's go." She took his hand and led him back to the research station, remarking on how she could no longer hear the sound of her toes squishing the moist sand beneath. There were some waves now, too, and the distant land masses could be seen now that the sun was out and the air was clear. From nowhere, the birds came to delight them with more sounds, while the tide continued to beat its steady rhythm.

"Tell me," she said. "What did you really do in the real world?"

He pursed his lips. "Actually, I was a stock broker."

She nodded. "I figured." □

Chapter Eleven

The Inviolate Rectitude of Human Life

"And you say the murder was almost perfect?" Ian McCormack leaned forward then, his entire persona caught up in the promise of a puzzle to be related. It was never particularly difficult to interest or to mystify poor torpid McCormack, but it was genuinely pleasing to Doctor Srinivas Malik when his friend displayed such guileless joy.

"No, I wouldn't say that, Ian. But it was well performed. Are you interested?" Malik crumpled his emptied plastic cream container, wishing desperately for the waitress to return with fresh coffee. That was the problem with the West: actual materials, luxuries and resources were far more plentiful and available, but the service was pitiful. He was never entirely immune to the culture shock, though he had had to make the transition from Malaysia to America -and vice versa- on many occasions before.

The briskness of this fall day, warm by midwestern standards, had startled him at first, as had the starkly tiled and antiseptic environs of the inhospitable cafe in which they now sat. The gaudy neon lights that adorned the streets of St. Louis were almost visible, now that the clouds had darkened considerably, reminding him of the nightclub strips of the polluted Asian megalopolis from which he had recently arrived. And so, Dr. Malik found himself surprisingly eager to recount his chimerical tale.

"Of course, Sri, of course. Start from the beginning, and don't leave anything out," McCormack implored.

"Oh, he won't leave anything out, Ian," Wei Chi added. "But I'm sure he'll throw in a few extras that really didn't happen."

"Don't worry, Wei, I'll make sure you get all the credit you deserve." Malik reached over to caress Wei Chi's slender left hand, feeling Octavius the rat squirming beneath Wei's silken sleeve. The pet rodent's presence probably violated all of the hospital's hygiene rules. But this trio had a fairly loose relationship with rules in general.

The late afternoon clouds of St. Louis receded then, revealing the glorious autumn sun straining to warm the earth as if the season were still summer. As the light threatened to fade again, shedding ominous portents of an undoubtedly frosty evening, Malik began to feel the appropriate chill in his bones, an apt sensation to accompany the tale of wickedness and murder into which he now launched.

The sky had been similarly overcast in Georgetown, Penang, on the evening of account. It was a day not unlike others passed on the historic Malaysian island, bathed in spicy guttural scents and eclectic street music that soothed the ear like wind-chimes. The hawkers bellowed their wares on the ancient streets, while priests from several prominent religions stood before their respective temples and shrines and endeavoured to beckon within any and all who passed.

Throughout it all, the majestic Komtar Tower, a hundred metres-high white cylinder that stood visible even from the Malaysian mainland, remained as unchanging as any Western shopping complex. Its many levels housed every kind of capitalist endeavour, from Bata Shoes to McDonald's, and from a complete modern hospital to some of the most high-priced condominiums available in Southeast Asia.

It was on this particular September evening that Dr. Malik had been summoned from the Komtar tower's hospital to tend to Mrs. Eunice Akimbe, an elderly woman who lived alone in one of the expensive Komtar condos.

It wasn't an emergency call, merely a request to drop in for tea and to discuss certain medical matters. That was the way Dr. Malik preferred to conduct business: over a hot beverage, and away from the sterility and death of white-washed hospital corridors.

"I like to deal with my patients on a social level," Malik explained to McCormack, "you know, so they don't feel overwhelmed by the hospital machine."

McCormack motioned for him to speed the telling of the tale. "So," he said, "you found her dead, right?"

Malik sighed and nodded, surprised by the potency of recurring loss he felt at the tale's re-telling. "Yes. I buzzed her door several times. When she failed to answer, Wei kicked the door down, and we found Mrs. Akimbe lying face-down in her bathroom, clothed only in a robe. And quite dead."

"Wait a minute. Wei was with you?" It was a silly question, and McCormack instantly retracted it. Malik never went anywhere without Wei Chi. She was, after all, far more pleasant than a switch-blade. Perhaps it was simple blatant paranoia that drove the mysterious doctor to seek

corporeal protection the likes of which Wei Chi so compe-
tently and lovingly provided. But McCormack suspected
a darker and more dubious aspect to his good friend's history and comportment. He had never found the courage
to ask.

It was indeed fortunate that Wei Chi had been by Malik's side, for the emotional surgeon was quite overcome
by the death of his patient and new friend. But after a few
moments of impassioned mourning, he brought himself
to inspect the body and its opulent surroundings.

It appeared as if Mrs. Akimbe had fallen forward off
of the toilet seat, though that could not be adequately
confirmed since her limbs were splayed awkwardly, and
since a brief examination of the toilet bowl revealed no
evidence of excretive bodily function.

McCormack squinted at this part of the story, but Malik gave him a disapproving stare. "Bodily functions are
nothing to get squeamish about, Ian. They are among the
few activities shared by all human beings, from beggars to
kings ...and even doctors."

The narrative continued: as Wei Chi telephoned the
police, Malik inspected the body. There were no obvious
wounds of any kind, except for the purple scars left from
her recent operation. Malik was, of course, intimately fa-

miliar with those blemishes since it was he was who had made the incisions from which the scars originated.

"From all indications," McCormack said confidently, "It sounds as if she just died of old age."

"Not quite," Malik countered. "She died of cardiac arrest. The autopsy confirmed that."

"Then it's not murder!"

Wei Chi laughed quietly at McCormack's certainty. Indeed, had Mrs. Akimbe not been an obscenely wealthy woman, her death would have been quietly noted by the authorities and forgotten, recorded as nothing more than an unfortunate heart attack. Malik had, after all, recently performed surgery on her to correct several clogged coronary arteries.

"I wouldn't say it's common," Dr. Malik explained, "But it's not unheard of for heart patients to die soon after their operations, from simply using the toilet." McCormack, once again, made a face. "It's odd, Ian," Malik continued. "The police inspector made that very same expression when I explained it to him. I am pleased to know that it's a universal response, and not a cause for medical concern."

"Well how does it happen? Sri, I just can't believe you can die from visiting the bathroom."

"From straining." Malik paused, thoughtful for a moment, perhaps recalling further unnamed medical tragedies. "When one strains over the toilet, one inadvertently raises one's intrathoracic pressure..."

McCormack made another face, one both Malik and Wei Chi recognized as the familiar look of confusion. "When you push too hard, your internal organs get squished together," Wei Chi explained.

"That's right," Malik confirmed. "And when that happens, your blood pressure also rises. That's what fighter pilots do to stay conscious when they're pulling high gees."

McCormack nodded.

"Anyway, Ian, your body likes to keep everything within a certain range. So, when you artificially raise your blood pressure like that, a few moments later your body will open up extra blood vessels in order to lower the pressure again to an acceptable level. Understand?"

McCormack nodded again, his mind no doubt riding a musky breeze back to some constipated fecal memory.

"So, when you suddenly stop straining," Wei Chi said, "the artificial elevation is removed, but those open vessels still remain..."

McCormack lurched forward abruptly, almost knocking tepid coffee all over the threesome. "Your blood pressure drops suddenly! Right?" An exultant Archimedal expression was enshrined preciously upon his cherubic face.

Malik smiled, pleased that his young imprudent friend was enjoying himself so, and gladdened beyond description that a fresh cup of coffee had arrived. Oddly, good coffee was one of the rarer commodities to come by in his journeys through the Far East. "Exactly. When that happens, for a brief moment there is insufficient venous blood returning to the heart. Thus, a weakened victim has a good chance of suffering a heart attack."

The Georgetown police inspector, a Mister Lumahn, had accepted Malik's description without much argument, even risking his own inspection of the toilet bowl. Curiously, someone else had already alerted the police of activities in the Akimbe condominium proximity, and Wei Chi's phone call had been redundant. Possibly it had been a concerned neighbour. But none of them admitted to the act.

"The thing is," Malik said. "Mrs. Akimbe was quite wealthy. You'd have to be to afford one of those condos in the Komtar tower. It seemed prudent for the police to be sure of no foul play."

"Hence the autopsy," McCormack offered. "I mean, your typical heart attack wouldn't warrant an autopsy, right?"

"That's right," Malik confirmed. "Like I said, the cause of death was cardiac arrest. But the bowels were empty, so it seems unlikely she had been straining over the toilet. And yet all indications pointed to a lack of venous blood return being the cause of the heart-attack."

"So..." McCormack reasoned slowly, "Someone must have induced a heart-attack, right? Unless Mrs Akimbe managed to flush the toilet before she died. But you did say it was murder."

"Yes," Wei said. "Forensic tests showed that someone may have come through the bathroom window at about the same time Akimbe died." McCormack's eyes widened. That was quite an important bit of information to suddenly add to the story!

Indeed, the East-facing window of Akimbe's condo was found opened some thirty centimetres. Interestingly, it had been Octavius, Wei Chi's pet rat, who had discovered the traces of sticky resin on the window sill. Octavius, sniffing about, had traced hints of the substance from the window sill and scattered about the bathroom and living room floors. The same diaphanous resin was later found on Mrs. Akimbe's throat, though there was no bruising.

In fact, there was no sign of a struggle at all, although the old woman was certainly not in a condition to offer resistance of any kind. There were no contusions, bruises or abrasions anywhere on her body, except for those explained by the recent surgery, and no fingerprints on the areas of her throat corresponding to the resin traces.

"So, she wasn't strangled?"

"No, Ian," Wei Chi explained. "When you strangle someone, you leave a bruise."

"Well, you would know, Wei. What do you think happened?"

"I know what happened," Wei Chi said. "Someone pressed her carotid sinus."

McCormack didn't have to say anything. It was clear from his resigned demeanour of medical and martial ignorance that he required some kind of expert assistance. Such physical honesty was one of McCormack's most endearing traits. It inspired such motherly concern from his friends that he was never at a loss for good conversation, friendly advice or a free meal.

"Allow me," Malik offered. "Here is my carotid sinus." Malik indicated the groove on his throat just adjacent to his trachea. "In this groove are various nerves that act as blood pressure sensors. If I press on my sinus, my brain thinks that my blood pressure has increased, and immediately acts to lower it..."

"And when you let go of the sinus, the bottom falls out of the system, and your blood pressure drops dramatically.

I think I get this stuff now." McCormack was ridiculously pleased with himself.

"Very good, Ian!" Malik was genuinely proud of his friend. He had always wanted to be a mentor to somebody. Why not McCormack? "Now, for most people, this isn't a big deal," Malik continued. "But for some, especially heart patients like Mrs. Akimbe, such a shift could be like straining on the toilet --deadly!"

"So, somebody poked her in the neck? No bruises? What about the condo? What else did the forensic people find?"

"Everything seemed in order, more or less," Malik said. "Except that one of the closets was in disarray, with the door wide open and a length of rope half pulled from it."

"Interesting. But that could be nothing, right? Mrs Akimbe could have done that herself."

"Possibly, Ian, but the rope also showed traces of resin, as did the inside walls of the closet."

McCormack sat back and digested these facts for a bit. His friends watched him in silence, content to observe his thought process. It was strangely calming. "Who could have had a motive?" He finally asked.

Malik was much gratified by McCormack's line of questioning. He had almost expected to find his American friends grown indolent and analytically barren from intellectually insulting television fare. Then again, as so much American television involved crime drama of some sort, perhaps insights into the criminal mind were indeed their forté.

By virtue of direct legal entitlement to Akimbe's money, three young men were singled out as suspects. All three were fraternal nephews of the late Akimbe, and all three projected comportments of pensive enmity, immediately failing to draw sympathy or laxity from the unforgiving Inspector Lumahn. It was therefore not entirely surprising when, against strenuous objections from the suspects' legal counsels, Malik and Wei Chi were granted unusual permission to observe the hastily convened interrogations. Being well positioned among the city's social elite did have its privileges.

The suspects had been gathered forthwith, and were assembled one-by-one before investigators morbidly within the living room of the late Mrs. Akimbe's Komtar condominium. Inspector Lumahn, it seemed, enjoyed melodrama as much as did Dr. Malik.

Joseph Akimbe was an Olympic-class weight-lifter, fallen on difficult times now that his major sponsors had backed out of an endorsement deal. A large man who spoke sparingly, he claimed to have been dining in one of the Komtar building's fast food establishments at the time of his aunt's death. There were no witnesses to corroborate his story.

Jacob "Anansi" Akimbe was a circus acrobat. Tightly muscular and agile, he was certainly an attractive figure of a man. He, too, was in dire financial straits since the carnival industry had been thumped hard by the global recession. It was his assertion that he had been shopping on the Komtar's mall level on the evening in question. But no one could substantiate his story, either.

The final suspect was Somerset Akimbe, a concert violinist. Of the three, his alibi was the tightest because he had been performing in a music hall before hundreds of spectators on the evening of the murder. However, he had had a full hour of intermission during which he could have easily walked to the Komtar tower, done the foul deed, then returned in time to finish the final musical set. Of the three, his financial need was also the greatest, having accrued an enormous debt from the purchase of antique violins on credit.

"Truly a rogues' gallery, " McCormack groused. His cherubic face took on yet another expression, this one similar to the earlier ones, but betraying a deeper level of perplexity. Within his brain, the hamster raced tirelessly on its wheel.

"According to the police reconstruction," McCormack asked, "did the killer enter through the bathroom window?"

Malik slapped his hands together in authentic gladness. "An excellent question, my friend! Again, it was Octavius who discovered that there was resin only on the inside handles of the window..."

"As if someone had opened it from the inside? But why, if indeed it was the killer who had done so?" McCormack thought for a second. "...Because only an acrobat could have climbed straight up the Komtar tower. Someone was trying to frame Anansi Akimbe?"

This time it was Wei Chi who smiled, though perhaps pleased more with her detective rat than with McCormack's cerebral windfalls. She caressed Octavius gingerly, demonstrating towards him much of the same affection she apparently held for Malik. "That would seem possible, Ian. But what of the resin?"

"Hmm," McCormack concentrated. "Resin the likes of which a weight-lifter might use to chalk his hands, or a violinist might use on his bow..."

"...Or an acrobat might use to improve his grip," Malik finished. The puzzle did not seem to be getting any easier.

Ian McCormack, an avid watcher of television crime drama, was intimately aware of the sensationalized aspects of police technology. The lack of hard scientific evidence in this case, though related to him second-hand, frustrated him profoundly. "Couldn't forensic tests discriminate between the three types?" he asked.

Again, Wei smiled, then laughed aloud. Westerners' perceptions of her homeland were always of one extreme or the other. Either they expected a metropolis of shantytowns whose technology had not risen above the neolithic, or they envisioned a shining Land of Oz with electronic toys rivalling the many playthings of effulgent Tokyo. Never could they imagine a thing somewhere in between. "The Georgetown police are very competent, and schooled in all the modern techniques," she finally said. "But they haven't the resources or the facilities for performing that kind of delicate forensic discernment, at least not so quickly."

Regardless, Octavius' little discovery had had dramatic consequences on the behaviour of the three suspects. To a man, each immediately changed his story when confronted by the finding, for fear that the resin traces, easily linked to any of the three professions, might lead to undesired conclusions.

"Before returning to the Komtar's lower levels for dinner," Joseph Akimbe, the weight-lifter, said in his new testimony, "I had actually stopped by to visit my aunt."

"Why didn't you mention this before?" Inspector Lumahn asked.

"Obviously," Akimbe said, "I was afraid. But I see now that only the truth can truly clear me of all suspicion."

"So what did you and your aunt do together?"

"Well," Akimbe began, pausing nervously, "We chatted. That's all. Perhaps for ten minutes. She complained that the air was getting stuffy, so I opened the bathroom window."

"Did you touch anything else?" Lumahn asked. "Did she offer you a drink or anything?"

"No! No. There was barely enough time. If it's finger prints you're after, I was wearing gloves the entire time. It was rather chilly that night."

"So," Lumahn continued, boring of the exchange, "why did you leave after only ten minutes?"

"She said she was expecting a social call from Dr. Malik." Akimbe stared at Malik then, his eyes burning accusingly into the doctor's own. Malik returned the stare nonplussed, even adding a trite raised eyebrow. Wei Chi had watched the exchange emotionlessly, assessing Akimbe's physique for structural defects lest she be called upon to physically defend her lover.

The next interview was with Somerset Akimbe, the concert violinist. He, too, admitted to having visited his aunt on the night of the murder. He had escaped from the concert hall during an intermission, and had raced over to spend a few minutes with her, as a good nephew should.

"We prayed," he said. "We are a Sunni family, though Auntie was far more religious than me. That happens when one is elderly and dying, you know; one senses one's mortality, and strives to forge a closer link with God."

Ian McCormack leaned forward at that point in the narration, his eyes twisted in characteristic, though engaging, puzzlement. "*Sunni?*"

"You Westerners!" Wei Chi pronounced with mild disgust. "So ignorant of other cultures! Sunni is one of the major branches of Islam. The Akimbes were Muslim."

"Oh," McCormack said, a bit embarrassed. "Of course. Do go on."

Somerset Akimbe's statement was sincere and well-articulated, much like the man. He insisted that he and his aunt had said a brief prayer, and that he had then returned to finish his recital.

Inspector Lumahn had yawned at that point, realizing that their interrogations had proceeded well through the night and into the next morning. He noticed Wei Chi shying from the glare of the rising sun as it shone through the wretched bathroom window, drawing his attention back to it. "And did you open the window, Mr. Akimbe?"

"Why yes," the violinist had replied. "Auntie likes to have a direct line of sight to Mecca, without buildings or panes of glass between her and the Holy City. I opened it so that we might pray, then I was careful to close it again before I left."

"Then why," Lumahn asked languidly, "did we not find your prints anywhere in this condominium?"

Somerset Akimbe simpered curtly, his talented fingers impatiently drumming the armrest of his chair. "I was between sets, Inspector. I need to keep my hands warm during intermission, so I always wear gloves at such times. I never take them off until the next set begins; not even for prayer."

At that point, Ian McCormack gurgled coffee from his mouth, and sputtered with insane chuckling. "You must be joking!" He accused. "I'll bet Anansi Akimbe came in wearing gloves, too, am I right?"

"No," Malik said calmly, taking the jittering cup from his friend's hand. "Anansi was wearing bandages over his fingertips. Seems he burned them while rehearsing some fire-breathing act. Claims to have put the bandages on himself, so there're no hospital records."

"And what was his story? Did he bring holy water to his ailing aunt's side, then open the window to let loose doves of peace?"

"Be serious, Ian," Wei Chi interjected. "Remember, Mrs. Akimbe was Sri's friend, not just another victim." McCormack calmed somewhat, perhaps a bit cowed. "Actually," Wei continued, "Anansi's story was rather interesting."

Anansi Akimbe, the acrobat, had diffidently offered his corrected deposition. With bandaged hands, he claimed to have banged on his Aunt's door at about the coroner's estimated time of death. He had not told the police of this before because he had feared that he would be in even greater suspicion.

"How did you know the time?" Lumahn asked.

"The elevators were broken," Anansi explained. "I had to climb the twenty flights of stairs. I looked at my watch when I got to the top because I like to time my athletic activities."

"How long did it take you?" Wei Chi asked, unsure of the protocol of intervening in someone else's interrogation. Lumahn wasn't certain if her question was related to the investigation, or was merely the curiosity of a fellow athlete. In any case, the Inspector did not interfere.

"I-I don't remember exactly..."

"But you remember the time it was when you got to the top?" Lumahn inserted.

"Yes, but that's only approximate, and only because Auntie's death..."

"How long did it take you --approximately?" Wei Chi asked again.

"I guess twelve minutes." Anansi then went on to describe how he had pounded on his Aunt's door several times, receiving no answer. He had then heard a light thump and nothing more.

"And did you call the police, Mr. Akimbe?"

"No, Inspector, I did not, and I am ashamed. I was afraid that if anything had happened to Auntie, I would be suspect. I wanted to be as far away as possible."

The narrative stopped there. Malik sipped his coffee patiently while Wei Chi watched Ian McCormack with sporting interest. he young man was clearly directionless, his many years of television sleuthing failing him dramatically.

"Is that it?" McCormack asked at last.

"Why yes, Ian," Malik answered. "Isn't it enough?"

McCormack pushed his coffee aside, frustrated, and surveyed the darkened streets through the cafe window. The Missouri night had fallen, and thousands of miles away a Malaysian day was just beginning, oblivious or uninterested in the malfeasance that had passed earlier. A murder had been committed, and all the alibis were reasonable, though suspicious. Where was the rub?

"Think, Ian," Wei offered. "One of the stories has a hole in it."

Malik finished his coffee and sighed loudly. "We didn't see it until we went out for a walk shortly after the interrogations," he said. "Wei and I were strolling through the Georgetown streets, looking at the tourist attractions: the temples, the shrines, the mosques..."

"Mosques!"

"Right, Ian," Wei took over. "We took particular interest in the *Kapitan Keling* mosque near the Komtar. Muslims were praying there, of course, but they were facing West."

"West?"

This time Malik laughed aloud. "Remember: Penang is East of Mecca, therefore a Malaysian Muslim must face to the West to pray!"

McCormack smiled in a distant, gawky manner. No doubt he was slowly putting it all together. "So Somerset Akimbe had lied! The window he had opened for prayer had been East-facing."

"That's right," Malik confirmed. "When confronted with his lie, he confessed. Seems he had tried to force Mrs. Akimbe to change her will that night. When she refused, he went to strangle her. But as soon as he touched her neck, her blood pressure dropped, and she died."

McCormack nodded. "And the window?"

"Well," Wei submitted, "it was as you first guessed, Ian. Somerset tried to frame his cousin Anansi. e was going to drape the rope from the closet through the window to make it look like a forced entry, but he was interrupted by Anansi's knocking..."

"...And dropped the rope! The light thump that Anansi heard?"

"Right," she continued. "So, he waited inside the closet until Anansi went away. Then he exited through the front door. e left the window open, and, in his panic, left the rope as it was, too. He also called the police to alert them to the fake break-in."

"Tragic," McCormack commented. "Truly tragic."

Malik nodded in agreement, casting his mind back to his years in Penang, and back to his deceased friend Mrs. Akimbe. A fine mystery was good entertainment for three comrades sharing a pot of coffee, but someone had really died. East and West were similar in at least one fashion: both cultures lacked the proper respect for the inviolate rectitude and dignity of human life. "It wasn't anywhere near a perfect crime," he said. "But it was a crime nonetheless." □

Chapter Twelve

The Emerald in
The Diamond

"Ian, ever wonder what Genghis Khan has to do with baseball?" Doctor Srinivas Malik selected his favourite Louisville Slugger from the rack, and warmly eyed the on-deck circle. Ian McCormack, still sweaty from a heartfelt ground-out, shook his head in response, wondering perhaps what odd twists and turns influenced the inconstant thoughts of his eternally distracted friend. "Well then listen..."

***

At the eastern end of the Silk Road, where camel caravans had struggled through exacting terrain of unpredictable temperament; where the forbidding peaks of the
snow-crested Pamir mountains teased the greedy with
their death-ridden passageways into rich and exotic medieval China; and where only the most driven of men
dared risk dissolution at the hands of thirst, clime or
brigands, there once rested a puissant Han citadel named
Khara-khoto, known to historians as the "Dark Fortress."

Long a focus of speculative lore in the area, and in
all ports serviced by the mighty Silk Road, shadowy
Khara-khoto was renowned for its impregnability, and for
its even darker mystery cached within. Its king, a swollen
thunderbolt of a man named Batur, was feared for his
ferocity, and respected for his integrity.

None who was not a citizen ever entered the gates of
the fortress-city. The caravans traded on the sand beds
beyond the bulwarks, where the grey-clad Khara-khoto
archers notched iron-tipped arrows and aimed them at any
foreigner in their sights.

Similarly, no citizen was permitted beyond the gates
unless sent on official business by despotic Batur. And yet
the rumours that thrived were fed on truth leaked from
between the blooded stones of the citadel's walls. Among
them were accounts of a vast unimaginable treasure of

gold, emeralds, jade and perfect silk stashed beneath the feet of iron-fisted Batur.

From this ample coffer the occasional token would suffice to purchase military might with which Batur could overcome any challenge of force that was offered him. And with the immense power that flowed from his treasure, from his brawny body and from his bellicose black-armoured troops, Batur held unwavering mastery over the rich multitude of desert kingships that surrounded him.

But all empires must fall, and it was destined that the reputation of mighty Batur would sooner or later become known to the most feared man in the world: Genghis Khan. Intent on stretching his predatory empire from the Pacific to Europe, and on subduing all men who dared challenge his dominance –even his dominance in reputation––the Great Khan set forth for the Dark Fortress, visions of Batur's glistening fortune lingering ghost-like in his eyes.

The Mongol Hordes came in force, for they did nothing half-way. Pillaging the fields as they came, they dispersed the allies of Batur and sent the despot an unmistakable message: Beware for the Great Khan has come.

Seeing the Asiatic horsemen galloping toward his city in the hundreds of thousands, Batur knew that not even he could hope to survive the ravages of Mongol vengeance.

They, too, were men of fame whose reputations for merciless and unrelenting destruction were founded upon undeniable fact. The Mongols never took prisoners.

And so Batur dressed in his finest black armour and drew his family to him. He took out his sword and slit the throats of his wife and children, rather than let them suffer Khara-khoto's unavoidable ruin and rapine. He then fought the battle of his life, falling inevitably before the bloody onslaught of the Hordes.

Yet Genghis Khan found no treasure within Khara-khoto, and so won no glory. In his rage, he razed the city to the ground, leaving nothing more than a pile of rock and bone to sleep forever in the wasteland of the fantastic Taklamakan desert.

"Nobody ever found the treasure?" Ian shouted to Malik who was just now commencing his warm-up swings near the on-deck circle.

"No, Ian, and the Chinese government has prohibited any investigation of the site."

"So..?"

"So where do I come in?" He swung jerkily, feeling the strength dwindle in his middle-aged arms, boyhood dreams of Major League glory now well forgotten. Only the promise of friendly charity games like this one still managed to spur that irreplaceable adolescent adrenaline rush. "At the hospital one day, back in Malaysia," he said, "I was fortunate to be present at the last rites of a dying man."

The man had been rushed from the airport to Malik's ward in Georgetown, Malaysia. Apparently, he had taken ill on an Air China flight bound for London from Beijing. Malik had arrived too late to do any good, and could only hold the dying man's hand while a Catholic priest heard the condemned' man's finl confessions.

McCormack scratched his head. "How come he died?"

"Well," Malik said, pausing in his warm-up for a moment, "It's not my field, but the best I could determine was that he had contracted a bizarre desert virus. Could have been anything. All kinds of nasty bugs in the Taklamakan desert, you know."

And, indeed, that was where the man had been. Ignoring the protestations and Latin rumblings of the doting priest, the dying man gazed into the piercing brown eyes of his doctor, and cried: "Batur's treasure! We found it!"

McCormack's eyebrows reached for his hairline. "It's true," Malik said, "the man, an Edmund North from Kent, England, claimed to have been part of an expedition three years ago. Seems he and two other Westerners were skulking about the Taklamakan..."

"Illegally?"

"You sound surprised that people do illegal things. Would that the world were as innocent as thou, my friend!"

"Well?"

"Of course, illegally! Khara-khoto's site is off-limits. But North claims that they found a handful of precious gems."

McCormack scratched his head. Malik wasn't sure if this was due to puzzlement or to his friend's disgustingly sweaty cap. McCormack's knotted forehead and pleading eyes gave him his answer. "One second, Ian. I'm up."

Malik strolled to home plate and eyed the pitcher, a startlingly attractive young Asian woman. Malik was not startled by her beauty as such, since she was after all his girlfriend Wei Chi, but by her unexpected expression of cool businesslike reserve and unfamiliarity. The Major League death stare had been adopted by an amateur, it seemed.

Malik took the first two pitches for balls, then fouled off the next two down the first-base line, just past the marble statue of baseball legend Chick Hayfee. e then felt his knees weaken somewhat as Wei Chi's slender white arm transformed itself into a medieval canon and erupted with such ferocity that Ted Williams himself would have hit the dirt. His bat barely flinched as a *shuto*, the wicked breaking pitch that Japanese ball-players fearfully call "the great equalizer," drilled deafeningly into the catcher's mitt for a called third strike.

"Well?" McCormack called to him as Malik ambled dejectedly back to the dugout. "Who were the other two guys?"

"What? Oh yes. In addition to North, there had been a Francois LaFontaine..."

"French?"

"Uh... I would assume so, Ian. nd a Gerald Charleton —an American from this very town, in fact."

"One of the guys was from St. Louis? You're kidding!"

"Why so surprised?" Malik asked playfully. "Are all Missourans as woefully ignorant of world history and geography as you?"

McCormack harrumphed and spat dutifully, but stuck to his line of questioning, teased and aroused by the promise of mystery and a puzzle to be solved. "So, what happened to the treasure?"

"An excellent question!" Malik poured himself a cup of GatorAid and settled back to watch Wei Chi devastate the remainder of their line-up. "They divided up the booty and scattered. North remained in China where he had taken a wife, while Charleton and LaFontaine came to St. Louis."

Wei Chi registered the third out of the final inning, ending their dismal charity game, then slinked over to offer her condolences. "Not too many tears I hope?" she said.

"Just tears of joy for your victory, my darling."

"Don't tell me," She guessed, "You're telling Ian about some mystery, aren't you, Sri?"

McCormack brightened and offered Wei a seat. "Mm hmm, it's really interesting. Seems there was this treasure in a place called Khara-khoto..."

"So has he gotten to the Chinese torture interrogation yet?" Wei Chi asked.

"What?!"

Malik laughed and pretended to throw his GatorAid into Wei Chi's open mouth. "Don't ruin my story! Or I'll have to hit a few homers off you next time..."

"When rhinos fly. Or when Ian gets a date."

"Hey!" McCormack interjected, "will someone please tell me about the Chinese torture interrogation?"

Wei Chi held her Malaysian doctor in a friendly head-lock, effectively preventing his speech. "Never underestimate certain governments, Ian," she said. "If you steal something valuable from the people who presently run the Chinese government --no matter to where you might escape-- expect to be brought back."

"Is that what happened to the three guys?"

"Yep," she said, loosening her grip on Malik somewhat. "Edmund North was already there, so he wasn't a problem.

But LaFontaine and Charleton were lured back with a faked letter from North."

The muffled voice of Srinivas Malik was faintly heard from beneath the underarm of the winning pitcher: "Remember that this was a couple of beers later..."

"What?"

"A couple of years later," he said, finally free of Wei Chi's compelling grasp. "North's share was recovered instantly, but the other two had already spent almost all of the rest of the wealth."

"Wastrels!" McCormack ejaculated. His companions stared at him for a brief moment, no doubt assessing the effect by association of Malik's unusual vocabulary on his impressionable young friend. It was a good effect, they decided.

"Indeed," Malik added cautiously, still enviously digesting the word *wastrel*. "But there was one item unaccounted for. It was a perfect emerald, the size of my palm."

"Wow. Some rock."

"Indeed," Malik said again. "The Chinese officials went to extreme lengths to encourage their guests to divulge the details of the gem's recent history."

McCormack glowered. "You mean torture, don't you?"

"Isn't that what I just said?"

"It's unreal," McCormack continued, "that people would do that sort of thing just for money."

This time Wei Chi frowned. She was eternally exasperated by the indignant naivete brandished by so many of her North American acquaintances. They seemed to squirm at the slightest suggestion of organic peculiarities or injuries. She measured her words mindfully. "Ian, physical discomfort has long been known to be a compelling impetus for cooperation."

"Ignore her, Ian," Malik said, "She beats people up for a living." He gestured to Wei's sheened deltoids, and was reminded of her martial adeptness, so effectively demonstrated on his head only moments earlier. "Besides, according to North, just the threat of torture was enough to get them to talk."

"And what did they say?"

"Ah! I thought you'd never ask!"

Trapped in an intimidating interrogation room with a score of grim-faced officials and humourless soldiers, just the PRC's reputation for ruthlessness was enough to loosen the Westerners' tongues. North had had little to say because his treasure had been recovered in its entirety almost immediately. But the stories of the other two were a bit more convoluted.

They both agreed that they had fled to St. Louis where
Charleton was a minor league baseball player.

"Ah!" McCormack cried. "The baseball connection."
Malik waved him to silence and continued his narration.

Together, Charelton and LaFontaine had pawned and
wasted almost all of Batur's ancient bonanza. When
pressed by the officials, LaFontaine --the weaker of the
two-- admitted that there had been one last prize unused:
the perfect emerald.

The jewel was about three centimetres by four centimetres, with about one centimetre of thickness. But its purity
and clarity of cut were unmatched, truly the work of a
long dead master. On one face was etched the portrait of
a desert horseman atop his steed; on the other side was a
drawing of a footprint, the most antediluvian representa-
tion of the Buddha. The relic would be prized by art and
history afficionados alike.

"Well?" McCormack pressed, "What happened to it?"

Wei Chi snickered guiltily, fearing playful retribution
from her lover. "Don't rush him, Ian," she said, "You know
how he likes melodrama."

Malik paused in his disclosure, levelling a slit-eyed stare
of disapproval at companion. "According to Charleton's
deathbed confession," he continued at last, "amazingly, the
two of them spotted the Chinese officials in the stands of

a ball game, just before the faked letter was delivered to them."

"So, they hid it."

"Don't get ahead of me!" Malik paused deliberately, feeling suppressed Thespian tendencies surfacing. He drew a sip of GatorAid and expressly measured the lapse, enjoying the drama perhaps a bit too much. "Fearing the worst," he said at last, "they hid the gem."

McCormack leapt to his feet and clapped his hands. "I knew it! That gem is somewhere in this park, isn't it?"

"Yes," Wei Chi said, "But where?"

The Missouran eyed the marble statue of Chick Hayfee suspiciously. "Betcha Chick knows."

"According to Charleton," Malik continued, "they sewed it into a baseball, hoping to retrieve it after the match. The ball was kept in play for most of the game, until Charleton himself came to bat. He hit it off the third base bag, and it bounced into the stands. He said that that was his second strike. His third was called on a fast ball, and he raced into the stands immediately afterward to find the original baseball..."

"...But it was gone." McCormack finished for him. "What a fool! Any normal man would have raced after that ball just as soon as it was fouled into the stands, or never have let it into the game at all."

Malik shrugged, eyeing the mystical baseball diamond and meditating serenely on the nature of the game. "He loved the game, Ian, as do many of us. Besides, if he had abandoned his at-bat after only two strikes, he would have caused some commotion, wouldn't you say?" The younger man shrugged and nodded.

"Tell him what the Frenchman said," Wei Chi offered.

"The Chinese weren't too happy with this version," Malik complied, "So they pressured LaFontaine for another story."

A snaky white finger was inserted into McCormack's collar to loosen its grip somewhat. He gulped audibly. "You mean... torture... don't you?"

"Yep. But he broke quickly. North told me that La-Fontaine kept screaming *'It's under the marble! it's under the marble'* right up until the end. I bet that lush French accent haunted him right up until..."

McCormack's face went pale. "What do you mean 'right up until the end'?"

Wei raised an eyebrow, perplexed again by her friend's lack of intestinal fortitude. "They killed him, of course," she said. "Both he and Charleton were shot for committing a capital archaeological offence." She took Malik's GatorAid from him, then added as an afterthought: "They knew what they were getting into."

"Yes," Malik added. "Their fates were sealed when agents here immediately looked beneath Chick Hayfee's marble statue and found nothing, not even a lost ball in the stands."

"And North?"

"Obviously he wasn't shot," Malik said. "He served a year in prison. Then they let him go because of his health. But he died in my hospital anyway."

The stands were empty now, as was the field since the other players had either gone home or were showering. Malik led his friends out onto the diamond, in a casual unrushed stroll.

"They knew that Charleton was lying right away," Malik explained. "They don't play much baseball in China. But they're not stupid."

"I don't get it," McCormack said.

"Oh, Ian, you do disappoint me sometimes. If a batter hits a ball onto the third base bag and the ball bounces into the stands, what's the call?"

"Foul ball?" McCormack offered tentatively.

"Ground rule double!" Wei exclaimed, quite pleased with her mastery of this foreign game. "The batter advances to second base, unaccosted!"

The realization sunk into the Missouran slowly. Charleton had lied, which gave strength to LaFontaine's testimony. "But what marble was he talking about?"

"LaFontaine was French and frantic," Malik said. "And I doubt if North knew any French at all. His friend wasn't saying 'it's under the *marble*'..."

"No?"

"No. He was saying: 'it's under the *marbre*.' That's French for 'home plate.'" Malik kicked home plate hard, then reached down to peel the bag from the field. There, revealed for three pairs of admiring eyes to see, was a perfect palm-sized emerald with an ancient drawing engraved on each side.

"As I do not fancy torturous retribution in any capacity," Malik said, "I shall take this promptly to the Chinese consulate." He then pocketed the gem wordlessly.

Wei Chi gestured to the batting cage and eyed her friends evilly, causing them to recall the brutal trouncing she had conferred upon their team earlier. "Batting practice anyone?" □

About the author

Raywat Deonandan is a multiple award-winning author of both fiction and non-fiction. Most notably, his 1999 collection of short stories, *Sweet Like Saltwater*, garnered the Guyana Prize for Literature (the national book award of the nation of Guyana) in the Best First Work category. Deonandan is a Professor at the University of Ottawa in Canada.

A Word from the Publisher

We hope you enjoyed this collection. If you did, we'd greatly appreciate it if you took time to write a positive review on the Amazon website. If you'd like to be kept abreast of future publications, including the opportunity to receive free books, please visit *Intanjible.com* and join our mailing list, or simply use your phone to scan the following QR code: